monsoonbooks

MOON KITE

Barbara Ismail spent several years in Kelantan in the 1970s and '80s, living in Kampong Dusun and Pengkalan Cepa, studying Wayang Siam and the Kelantanese dialect. She holds a PhD in Anthropology from Yale University, and is originally from Brooklyn, New York.

Moon Kite is the fourth in Barbara Ismail's series of Kain Songket Mysteries based in Kelantan. The first book in the series, *Shadow Play*, won Best Debut Novel at the 2012 SBPA Book Awards in Singapore and was shortlisted for the Popular–The Star Readers' Choice Awards 2013 in Malaysia; the second book in the series, *Princess Play*, was shortlisted for the Popular–The Star Readers' Choice Awards 2014 in Malaysia.

For more information about the author and her books, visit *www.barbaraismail.com*.

Kain Songket Mysteries
(published and forthcoming)

MOON KITE

Volume IV in the Kain Songket Mysteries Series

BARBARA ISMAIL

monsoonbooks

First published in 2017
by Monsoon Books Ltd
www.monsoonbooks.co.uk

No.1 Duke of Windsor Suite, Burrough Court,
Burrough on the Hill, Leicestershire LE14 2QS, UK

First edition.

ISBN (paperback): 9781912049028
ISBN (ebook): 9781912049035

Cover design by Cover Kitchen.

A Cataloguing-in-Publication data record is available from the British
Library.

Printed in Great Britain by Clays Ltd, St Ives plc
20 19 18 17   1 2 3 4 5

For
Ashikin Mohd. Ali Flindall and Zainal Bakri Mohd. Ali

Malay Glossary

Adik: Younger sibling.

Adik-adik: Younger siblings.

Alamak: A cry of surprise.

Ayah: Father.

Ayam Percik: Chicken grilled with a thick coconut sauce: a Kelantan specialty.

Batik: Cotton stamped or drawn with wax print designs, made in Kelantan, Malaysia and Indonesia.

Bomoh: Magical Practitioner.

Che: Mister.

Cik: 'Miss' or 'Mrs'.

Fajr: Dawn; the dawn prayer, the first of the day.

Jampi: Magic spell.

Kain Pelikat: Plaid cotton used for a man's sarong.

Kain Songket (or Songket): A fabric of woven silk with geometric designs made of gold. Kelantan is famed for the quality of its *songket*.

Kakak: Older sister, also used between two older women.

Kampong: Village.

Kerbau: Water Buffalo.

Keris: Wavy bladed Malay dagger.

Maghrib: The prayer at sundown.

Main Puteri: A spirit exorcism performed to dancing and music. Literally means 'Princess Play'.

Mak: Mother.

Mak Cik: Auntie, a polite address for a woman older than the speaker.

Merbok: Zebra Dove, prized for singing.

Nasi Lemak: Rice with a side dish of curry (usually chicken or fish) and a vegetable, wrapped up in a single serving banana leaf.

Nenek: Grandmother.

Onde-onde: A type of Malay cake made of sweet rice flour with a palm sugar center, covered in coconut flakes.

Padi: Wet rice plant.

Parang: Machete.

Pasar Besar: Main Market.

Pondan: Homosexual, particularly transvestite.

Ringgit: Malaysian currency.

Sarong: Tubular skirt covering the wearer from waist to ankle. For both men and women: men's are plaid, and women's batik, for the most part.

Semangat: Soul, energy.

Tahi Itek: Literally 'duck faeces'; a kind of Malay cake made with custard.

Talak: A pronouncement of divorce. Talak are cumulative, and after one or two talak a couple can remarry, but after three, the woman must marry someone else first before she can remarry her former husband.

'Tok: From *Datok*, grandfather.

Tukang Wau: Kite maker, a respected and intricate craft.

Wau Bulan: Literally 'Moon Kite', a popular shape of competitive kite.

Malay Idioms

Bagai kunyet dengan kapur

Like turmeric and lime: both of which are necessary to form a betel nut quid.

Bawa perut kerumah orang

To carry your stomach to someone else's house: to cadge a meal.

Bertukar jiwa dengan semangat

To exchange your soul for your life force: a terrible bargain.

Duduk seperti kucing, melompat seperti harimau

To sit like a cat and spring like a tiger.

Harimau menyembunyikan kuku

The tiger hides his claws: hiding one's true nature.

Katak dibawah tempurong

A frog under a coconut shell: someone who knows little of the outside world.

Kerbau cucok hidung

Like a buffalo with a ring through its nose: easily led.

Laksana katak: sikit hujan, banyak bermain

Like a frog, getting much joy from a little rain. Someone easily pleased.

Macam itik mendengarkan guntur

Like a duck listening to thunder: understanding nothing about what he hears.

Macam kuku dengan isinya

Like the nail and the quick: inseparable friends.

Menyokong padi nak rebah

To prop up *padi* (rice plants) about to fall. The kind of support friends provide to each other.

Pelandok lupa jerat, tapi jerat tak melupakan pelandok

The deer forgets the trap, but the trap doesn't forget the deer. The law will trap a criminal eventually.

Penyu bertelor ber-riburibu, seorang pun tak tahu, ayam bertelor sebiji pecah khabar sebuah negeri

A turtle lays thousands of eggs and no one's the wiser, a chicken lays one and tells the whole world.

Potong hidung, rosak muka

Cut off the nose and destroy the face: the disgrace of one member can destroy the whole family.

Rambut sama hitam, hati masing-masing

We all have black hair, but each has its own heart. You can't tell what someone is thinking.

Seperti parut di muka, puru di bibir

Like the scar on your face or the sore on your lip: a situation which must be accepted.

Tempat gajah lalu

Where an elephant passed: total destruction.

Upah bidan pun tak terbayar

Not worth the midwife's fee. A wicked child.

Yang rebah, di tindeh

Whoever falls is stepped on: if you are down you will remain down.

Chapter I

Everyone's eyes were drawn to the sky, peering at the battling kites swooping above them. These were large Kelantanese fighting kites, elongated ovals with a crescent moon below: *wau bulan,* moon kites. They flew on strings coated with ground glass, to more effectively cut an opponent's kite loose, taking them out of the game.

In many areas of the world, so Maryam understood, kite flying was a children's pastime, the purview of amateurs and toddlers, and the kites themselves flimsy, plain and cheap. In Kelantan, Maryam was proud to think, kites were a serious business, from their inception in the workshops of *tukang wau* and their painstaking decoration, to their handling by skilled flyers who'd spent years perfecting their abilities. No toddlers dared to touch these kites, expensive and beautifully put together as they were. This was an adult activity, and, as with so many Kelantanese competitions, a great deal of money was often riding on the outcome.

Maryam's husband, Mamat, was a songbird fancier, and that hobby took up most of his spare time: that is, time remaining after coffeeshop gatherings, acting as a father and grandfather and helping Maryam with her business. There were, as he explained to Maryam, who knew this already all too well, just so many hours in the day and one couldn't be an expert at everything. They were occasional spectators rather than participants or even fervid fans: happy enough to watch the kites fly over dry rice fields if they had time, otherwise, happy to pay no attention at all. Their youngest son, Yi, now in high school but still gangly and sometimes alarmingly awkward, liked kites and was interested in them, but hadn't ever participated in a contest.

During the dry season, contests were held in the padi fields, which changed from muddy swamps to dry, cracked land. The wide-open spaces were perfect for contests, giving the flyers plenty of room to run their kites, and room for spectators, too. All eyes had been looking up, at the kites and the sky, so it was a longer time than one would have thought before anyone noticed something large swinging from a tree.

* * *

Nik Man was a long time kite flyer, having begun his career as a boy, following the men who flew kites in all the competitions, acting as their aide-de-camp and learning the skills by watching and osmosis. He'd always loved kites: at first it was the designs, and the colours and shapes which drew him. And then, as he grew older, it was their flight, their freedom and swooping, and the fighting going on between them. In fierce rivalries, flyers sought to cut each other's kite free, using ground glass on their kite strings. Setting a kite free not only won the contest at hand, but deprived an opponent of a considerable investment, affecting his future performance. There was a lot to consider in a competition, and Nik Man appreciated it all.

Nik Man grew up in Kampong Banggol, farther up the Kelantan River from Kota Bharu, towards the coast. Though enthusiasts came from all over Kelantan and many different villages, Kampong Banggol was a hotbed of kite flying, and it seemed every male in town flew kites, made them, or at least had strong opinions on the subject. Where in other places coffeeshop talk might have centred on politics or local football, Kampong Banggol discussions focused on kite flying, and an adroit listener could learn a lot just keeping quiet and drinking his coffee.

Nik Man's companion in this endeavour, his Sancho Panza, was Idris, known to all as Dris, a friend since childhood from the same village. Where Nik Man was active in his interest, Dris was a follower, who tagged behind his friend acting as a general helper and gofer. When Nik Man was the apprentice, Dris was the apprentice's apprentice, and so it had always been, though now they were well into adulthood, each with families of his own. Even into maturity, the dynamic between them had not changed, and Dris still, as a grown man, appeared to be tagging after Nik Man, who never took on a boy as his helper, but had Dris in the same position he'd been in since their school days.

Nik Man was good, very good, and often a winner in competitions. Due to his status as a player, he had backers: men who bet large amounts on the competitions and expected Nik Man to win. Almost all the spectators at an event bet on the outcome – even the competitors usually bet on themselves, and a good deal of money changed hands at these events. While it was not Nik Man's only source of income, as he also owned rice land that he farmed, it was a decent percentage of it, and one he would do a great deal to protect.

Most of the competitors knew each other, and had been flying together for many years. It was rare for an adult to suddenly enter the lists, since the approved method of learning the skill was to apprentice, but it did occasionally happen. When it did, the other professionals were usually unimpressed, and did not expect to see that flyer for long. If they were not ready or able to commit to the skill in childhood, there was no reason to believe they could do so as adults, when the odds were stacked against them.

This competition, held in a dry rice field near the village of Kampong Penambang, a centre of *kain songket* weaving, featured just such a newly minted expert named Salim, also from Kampong Banggol, a man fervently detested by his neighbours at the competition. Where Nik Man had laboured for years to reach his position, this Salim had various enthusiasms, which he pursued for a time and then dropped. Which would be fine, as far as Nik Man and others were concerned, as it was no business of theirs how he wanted to waste his time and money, but Salim could be unbearable. He took any beginner's luck, or winning by mistake, as proof of his own genius and crowed about it to anyone who'd listen. At the same time, he'd take the opportunity to degrade others who'd toiled in that particular vineyard, telling them to their faces how well he'd done when they were unable to beat him. And of course, he ascribed it all to his own skill, virtuosity even: conceiving of his victory, as a fluke would never have occurred to him.

He was not only cordially disliked, but avoided for his uncertain temper, which flared quickly and often violently, and had already cost him several marriages (and might well cost him his current wife). For a man his age, in his early forties, it was surprising to see such childish behaviour, but as more than one person had commented, he would never learn and probably never grow up, since he hadn't already.

Therefore, when the kites took the field, Salim's presence was greeted with gritted teeth and averted eyes, as the professional flyers sought to ignore him and concentrate on their games. He was loud and obnoxious and, of course, had no acolytes – it was hard to imagine the parent who would allow his son to follow Salim around and learn from him – and the best that could be hoped for was that he would lose early and go home. Sadly, even for him, this was not to be, and in a shocking development, he cut Nik Man's kite string, knocking him out of the competition and losing his kite.

Nik Man looked up at his kite soaring away from him, not to be recovered, in disbelief and welling anger. Salim, ignoring all rules of sportsmanship, not to mention basic courtesy, was gloating over his triumph, which Nik Man considered more of an accident, grinning like an idiot and hooting like an ape. Completely unnecessary, since everyone saw it, and most pretended they did not, so as not to encourage Salim or embarrass Nik Man. But Salim would not let it go.

Nik Man walked stiffly back to the trees on the side of the field to his waiting sidekick, Dris, who hung about him anxiously waiting for a comment. It came, unprintably, while Nik Man dried his face with a towel and looked angrily, yet sadly, at the sky as if his kite might drift back down to him. 'Why can't he shut up?' he asked no one in particular, but it was clearly a painful moment. Nik Man decided, in the face of what happened, to leave the contest and go home, away from his loss and from the fool who'd beaten him. As Dris gathered his things, he noticed Omar standing along the side: Omar, the *bomoh* from his own kampong who provided his kite magic designed to avoid just such an outcome as he had just had.

'Why are you here,' Nik Man demanded, not even bothering with the niceties of 'good morning', or 'how are you'. 'What are you doing here?' Omar never came to competitions, even though he provided the magic, and Nik Man could not imagine why he was present now.

Omar looked startled to see him, although why that should be he couldn't imagine. 'Nik Man,' he identified him. 'Oh.'

'What are you doing here?'

'I, I came to see you fly.'

'Really? Why?'

'Just so,' he said with an ingratiating smile. 'You know, I thought I don't usually go to see you, and I work to give you the *jampi* you need so I thought I'd see how it worked.' He smiled again.

'Not too well,' Nik Man informed him. 'I just had my string cut by Salim,' he hissed the name. 'The whole kite's gone.'

'Oh, I'm sorry. I saw it.'

'Yeah. You know, I know no jampi can work all the time, but I would have given a lot for it to have worked now, so I wouldn't have to hear Salim talking about how wonderful he is.'

Omar looked uncomfortable. 'I know, it's too bad. Well, there's always next time.'

Nik Man nodded, unconvinced, and looked back at the kites.

'Are you going home?' Omar asked hopefully.

Nik Man nodded again, but seemed to be engrossed in the competition. Omar moved from one foot to the other, seemingly impatient for Nik Man to be off, though Nik Man took no notice of him. 'Look at that,' he murmured to Dris, who stood next to him. 'Nice move,' Dris agreed, and they both stood, arms crossed over their chests, in the same stance, though neither of them realized it. Omar began to walk away, apparently unable to stand near them without fidgeting, and was soon lost among the other spectators.

At the end of the contest, Salim had won. Instead of accepting it modestly, as almost all winners did, he smiled and talked incessantly about his conquest, with his fellow flyers moving away to stand together against him. They spoke in low voices to each other about how horrible he was, how he had no manners, no sportsmanship and no talent. 'It was an accident,' said one man sourly, 'and I wouldn't mind an accident, but him? I can't listen.'

Everyone seemed to agree heartily with this assessment, and Nik Man watched as Salim jubilantly walked to the crowd, who either ignored him completely or watched him guardedly. He seemed completely unaware of this, searching through the crowd until he located Omar, around whom he threw his arms while exulting. 'Did you see it? Amazing, right?' He laughed and pounded Omar on the back, while Omar looked guiltily around him. He met Nik Man's questioning gaze and had the grace to blush.

Nik Man and his faithful Dris strolled over to the victor, who was giving Omar and anyone within earshot the blow by blow commentary on how he'd succeeded and why: a combination of natural talent, deserved luck and brilliant jampi, which he, Salim, chose and directed, and Omar provided.

Nik Man stood in front of Omar saying nothing, but pinning him with a glare. 'The jampi you gave him?' Nik Man waited for an answer.

Omar answered nervously. 'Just a couple, you know. Not like what I give to you. Just a couple.'

'Why are you dealing with him at all?'

'He asked me.' Nik Man did not seem impressed. 'You know, maybe I shouldn't have, but I did. I'm sorry. Now that I think about it, maybe I shouldn't have.'

'Now that you think about it,' Nik Man repeated.

'I'm sorry. It won't happen again.'

'Perhaps I need another bomoh. One who won't look to make money off anyone else who asks him.'

'No, it's not …'

Salim came up to them, grinning. 'You didn't know,' he teased Nik Man. 'He gave me jampi too, and now I'd say he gave me the better ones! Maybe because he saw the real talent in me!'

Nik Man looked ominously at both Salim and Omar, turned on his heel and walked off. Salim flung his arm around Omar, who shook it off and trotted after Nik Man. Salim looked hurt for a moment, and then his face cleared and took off after them both as they entered the trees on the border of the field. And a few minutes later, that's where Salim's body was found, swinging from a tree by a glass-coated kite string.

* * *

A teenaged boy called nervously from the bottom of Maryam's steps, politely keeping to the ground until he was invited up, while trying to fend off the attacks of beady-eyed geese without inflicting any injury on them. Maryam came to the door and shooed away the birds to rescue her visitor and invited him up, though she'd never seen him before.

He introduced himself shyly, and pointed vaguely towards the road. 'They said to call you, Mak Cik,' he explained without clarification. 'There's something there that maybe you could …' He ran out of steam at this point, with Maryam none the wiser as to why he had appeared. Without answering, she descended the stairs and prepared to follow him; since clearly nothing would be explained until she arrived at wherever he was talking about.

At a nearby field, the crowd heaved before a large tree, and kites lay on the ground forgotten. This in itself was alarming, as enthusiasts never simply abandoned their kites, but treated them with tender regard. She wormed her way through the throng of people, bending forward and murmuring 'excuse me' without ceasing, until she stopped short at the front, staring directly at a man's body swinging from a kite string, coated with ground glass, tied to the tree. 'Alamak!' she cried involuntarily, her shock holding her still.

The woman next to her nodded. 'I sent him for you,' she indicated the boy who'd come for Maryam with her chin. 'I know you'll know what to do, being a detective and all.' She smiled at Maryam approvingly, and patted her softly on the shoulder. 'You'll find out whatever is ... necessary.'

'Do you know who he is?' Maryam looked more keenly at the body now, trying to see the man's age and features.

'Of course!' the woman replied confidently. 'It's Salim, from Kampong Banggol. He won today! It was a real surprise. He's new at this, just started flying, and he beat some of the best here. But now, this ...' She seemed to lose her poise, but it was only momentary – Kelantan women did not crumble. 'I can't imagine ...' She stammered to a stop.

Maryam moved closer to the tree. She could see now Salim was in his forties, stocky, a bit short, with broad shoulders. He looked strong and quick – well, he'd have to be, to be a kite flyer. A traditionally tied cloth covered his hair to keep it out of his eyes, and he wore a sarong and a T-shirt, together with sturdy sneakers, which looked out of place under a traditional sarong, but it was a practical outfit for the activity at hand. 'Does he have a family?' she asked, staring at the man, wishing she could cut him down and lay him out decently.

'A wife, I know. That's all.'

'Is she here?' Maryam turned from the body and toward the crowd. 'Call the police in Kota Bharu!' she said loudly, and was gratified to see a few men leave the crowd and follow her orders. 'Do you see her?' She asked the woman again.

The woman pointed at another woman standing with a few

men, waiting calmly to see what happened now. She didn't look in the least bit upset, though her face was a bit puffy around the eyes. Maryam doubted it was tears; this woman wasn't even near to tears, and she wondered what it could be.

Chapter II

Osman, the Police Chief of Kota Bharu, the highest-ranking
Police officer in the state of Kelantan, stepped down from
his car and warily eyed the swinging body and the restive crowd
in front of it. He hated finding bodies, but now, looking at this
new one, he decided he hated hanged bodies more than any other
type. There was something so eerie about seeing it suspended
there: he could barely look at it without shivering. The crowd
began melting away, as though the tide went out, taking with it
everyone in the field. Osman walked over to the widow, when she
was pointed out to him. He smiled and introduced himself.

'Halimah,' she said shortly, drawing her head cloth tighter
around her shoulders. She stood with three other men from her
kampong, introducing them as Nik Man, Dris and Omar. They
nodded nervously at Osman and stayed silent.

'I'm so sorry for your loss,' Osman said, though it seemed he
was wasting his breath offering sympathy. She looked completely
calm. She nodded her thanks and stood there waiting for him to
ask anything.

'Did you see anything?'

'No.'

'Were you here to watch him play?'

'Yes,' she answered shortly.

'Did he often fly kites?'

She shook her head. 'He was new to this. He really just started doing it.'

'Did you always come to watch him?'

'No. Just today.'

'Why?'

She shrugged, and left it at that.

Osman looked around at the group, wondering why they had all stayed. 'Let's go to talk,' he said, and asked Maryam if they could adjourn to her porch.

Leaving the others on the porch, fortified with Rubiah's cakes and coffee, Osman began with Halimah, the preternaturally composed widow. He too noticed her face was swollen: was it bruised? He couldn't tell, and she was not volunteering.

'How long have you been married?' he started quietly.

'About three years,' she said.

'Has it been a happy marriage?' He felt like a fool asking a question like that, but he had to introduce the topic somehow. He glanced over to Maryam for help, and she returned his look.

'Not ... I don't know. We'd had our problems,' she said candidly. No use pretending – if she didn't tell him someone else in the kampong would, and then it would look worse. She took a deep breath. 'We've already been divorced with two *talak*. He had a terrible temper.' She looked directly at Osman.

'I see,' he faltered. 'So did he, your face, I mean ...'

'He did try to hit me this morning. As I said, a very bad temper. *Upah bidan pun tak terbayar*: A boy not worth the midwife's fee.

I had already made up my mind to leave. I have children and grandchildren. I don't have to stay there. What kind of a person would I be to accept this kind of treatment?' Osman wasn't sure she was talking to him, exactly. Next to him, Maryam nodded, encouraging her. 'I was actually there to tell him I was through. But I never got to tell him, because before I could speak to him someone had killed him.'

'Do you have any idea who might have wanted to kill him?'

She smiled a mirthless smile. 'Many people,' she informed him. 'He had a rotten temper. Not always. At the beginning of our marriage he really tried, and it was fine. But he can't keep it up, you see. So we ended up here. I imagine …' she continued, pulling out hand-rolled cigarettes from her sarong. Maryam smiled at her, motioning for her to put them down, and commandeered Mamat's Rothmans. Halimah smiled her thanks. 'I imagine there were plenty of people who had a grudge against him. Probably plenty of them at the contest.'

'He was killed there,' Osman noted, 'so most probably it was one of them.'

Halimah looked amused. 'Probably one of the people you've got here,' she agreed. Osman was not prepared for one of his suspects to concur so readily. She understood the look on his face. 'I'm only saying what you already know. Would it help if I pretended not to know? Or pretended I'm terribly upset that he's gone? He's acted badly for the past year at least, maybe more, and that's given a lot of people reason to hate him.' She peacefully smoked her cigarette and waited for Osman to think of another question.

'Were you with anyone while you were at the contest?'

'Not really. I came to tell him I'm leaving, and I hadn't meant to do it front of a lot of people. I could have, though.' She thought about it. 'I just saw all the people from my kampong, Nik Mat and Dris and Omar, and stood with them after the body was found.'

'So they don't know where you were …'

'And I don't know where they were when the deed was done. Correct.' And she continued smoking. Osman looked helplessly at Maryam, not knowing where to go with that.

'We'll get back to you,' Maryam said cheerfully. 'Would you mind waiting outside?'

* * *

Nik Man was next, and he too, looked relatively unruffled for a man being interviewed in a murder case.

'How were you doing? In the contest, I mean,' Osman turned his eyes for the first time to the man in front of him.

Nik Man took a deep drag on his cigarette before answering. 'Not so well,' he shrugged. 'Worse than usual. The wind somehow wasn't with me today; it seemed to be fighting against itself. You know,' he began to speak more fluently as he explained his passion, 'I just couldn't seem to get the kite going right, and couldn't get to the other kites to cut them down. Some days it just doesn't happen as it should. I don't know …' He looked thoughtful.

'How about Salim?' Osman continued.

'Oh, he was doing great! Really, it was just his day. The kite was high and fast, really moving. Yes, it was his day. He won!'

Then he thought about it, and added, 'It was almost an accident, though. He didn't really know what he was doing, but he cut my kite and I lost.'

'Were you upset about it?'

Nik Man looked at his cigarette. 'You can't be upset every time you don't win,' he explained calmly. 'It's part of competing: you can't win every contest. But this was different because Salim was so petty, yes, that's the word, when he won. Crowing about it, preening, bragging. It isn't done; you don't rub people's faces in losing, because next time it will be you. But he knew nothing about competing, and so he was terrible. He made us all so angry.'

Maryam drew Osman aside, and looked around furtively before speaking.

'You don't think he was killed because he was winning a kite flying contest, do you?' She demanded.

Osman shrugged and looked tired. 'I've seen sillier reasons to kill someone. *You've* seen sillier reasons. Why not a kite competition?'

He turned back to Nik Man. 'Did you have words with Salim?'

'Not really. What is there to say? He knew what I thought of him.'

'Was there anyone else you were upset with?'

Nik Man considered it. 'Omar. Omar betrayed me.'

Osman was shocked. 'Why? What did he do?'

'Omar was my bomoh. I don't mean mine for everything, but I used him for all my kite flying jampi. I paid him every month. And I thought he was loyal to me. I thought he wouldn't provide any jampi for anyone else.'

'Are there kite flying jampi? I'm just asking ...'

Nik Man stared at him. 'Of course there are. Everyone uses them.'

'Of course,' Osman muttered. 'Please go on.' He believed Kelantanese had magic mixed up in everything. The fact that he always found it involved in his cases hardly gave him any reason to disbelieve it.

'Anyway, I paid Omar quite a lot, every month, to provide me with jampi for my kites. And then, when Salim won, do you know what he said? He said thanks to Omar, for his jampi. I couldn't believe what I heard. Omar said maybe he shouldn't have done it. That's right, he shouldn't but he did. Just to make a little more money, he'd lose me altogether. I couldn't believe it! I still can't believe it. Salim will give up on this just like he does everything else.' He thought about what he'd just said and restated it. 'If he were alive, he would never have stuck with this and then Omar would have lost me and never had Salim. What was that? Why would he do it? I still don't know.'

'But it was Salim who let you know?'

Nik Man nodded. 'Yes, because he thanked him. Otherwise I wouldn't have suspected, although ... I was really surprised to see Omar there. He never comes to contests. Maybe I would have thought about it and then come to it eventually, but I wouldn't be talking about it now.'

'Do you have any ideas on why someone would kill Salim?'

Nik Man smiled. 'Anyone would want to kill him. And someone actually did.'

Chapter III

Dris seemed the paradigm of a good-natured kampong man. He was on the porch of Maryam's house and began collecting his cigarettes and coffee to enter the living room. 'Terrible thing,' he commented as he entered.

'How long have you known Salim?'

'I've known him forever. Neighbours. Went to school together. We both grew up in Kampong Banggol, with Nik Man.'

'And you all like kites?' Maryam asked.

'Well enough,' he answered. 'Nik Man has the talent, not me. But I help him,' he said proudly. 'You need help to keep your stuff together. But, yes, we both liked it – most men in Kampong Banggol do.' He shrugged and picked up his coffee cup.

'Do you work with him on all his kites?'

Dris nodded. 'Yes, I do.'

'Why were you helping him like that?' Osman asked.

Dris seemed surprised. 'He's my friend, why not? It's not as much fun getting your kite ready all alone.' He looked at Osman with some pity, since from his question it seemed he might not have many friends.

'But you don't always get paid, do you?'

Dris shifted uncomfortably. 'Well, it wasn't really an official job,' he replied. 'No, more like two friends doing something together they really liked.'

'But Nik Man was paid when he won,' Osman observed.

'Yes, he bet on himself. Of course he got paid.'

Maryam leaned in, unfamiliar with the financial aspects of kite flying. 'How else does one get paid to fly kites?'

'Well, other people bet on you too. There are a lot of fans, you know. And then if they win, they pay you too.'

'So Nik Man could make quite a good living kite flying.'

'He also had some rice land,' Dris was quick to assure her. 'He made money kite flying but I don't know if it's really a lot.'

'But you made less.'

'Of course. I didn't fly the kite. I just helped.'

'Does everyone have a helper?' Osman asked.

Dris shrugged. 'Not everyone. But I think you need one.'

'What else do you do?' asked Maryam. She didn't always expect men to 'do' anything, but they still had to contribute.

'I have rice land. I help my wife at the market, you know.'

She nodded. Many Kelantanese men were like that, holding various jobs at various times, and always ready to help their wives at the market. Her own husband, Mamat, did the same, but she didn't think of him that way – she thought of him as gainfully employed.

'Did you use kite magic? Jampi?' Osman asked suddenly. Maryam sighed.

'Yes, we did,' Dris gave Osman a look such as one would give the terminally dim witted. 'Everyone does.'

Osman nodded. 'Which *bomoh* did you use?'

'Pak Omar. He lives here. He had an arrangement with Nik Man. He provided all the jampi and wrote them on the kites and all of that, and Nik Man paid him every month.'

'On retainer?' Osman asked, but Dris looked at him blankly.

'Was Nik Man unhappy with Omar that you know of?'

Dris' eyes clouded. 'Oh, Salim of course. He was announcing his win and how great he was. *Penyu bertelor ber-riburibu, seorang pun tak tahu, ayam bertelor sebiji pecah khabar sebuah negeri:* A turtle lays thousands of eggs and no one's the wiser, a chicken lays one egg and tells the whole world. That was Salim all over. Then he started thanking Omar for giving him jampi. I could see Nik Man go white hearing it. You know, if you're paying a bomoh like this, I mean every month, to keep up your jampi, he isn't supposed to work with anyone else. Especially someone like Salim.'

'Why would it do it?'

Dris shrugged. 'Greedy, maybe. A few extra dollars. I can't imagine.'

'Could it help his business?' Maryam asked.

'Maybe.' Dris thought about it. 'But then, people would know he let Nik Man down, and who would want to use someone who would do that? It's just stupid.'

'Could Salim have threatened him?' Osman asked.

'I hadn't thought of that,' Dris admitted. 'But Omar is a grown man. You can't let people just threaten you like that.' He looked up at both of them. 'Are we done now? I need to go home.'

* * *

'No one seems that upset, you have to agree,' Maryam said to Osman, clearing some plates to make room for their last guest, Omar. 'It's hard to imagine anyone leaving a less grieving group behind them.'

'He must have been something,' Osman agreed. 'Even when they're trying to be nice they can't say anything better than "at least he's dead". I hope I get more when I leave this world.'

'You absolutely will,' Maryam assured him, smiling. 'Your children will be missing you terribly.' Osman blushed, as Maryam well knew that Osman and his wife Azrina were hoping for a baby soon, and Maryam suspected it would be sooner than they realized. Besides, Osman was well loved by his wife, family and Maryam and her family, and though she hoped this would not come up as an issue for many years, those who knew him would sorely miss him. As Maryam hoped she herself would be missed, and as Salim clearly would not.

Omar was a poised and more polished presenter than the other three, but no less calmer than they. Omar greeted them with a professional smile. As they began to talk, his smile faded and he began to look grave.

'It's a sad business,' he commented mournfully. 'While kite flying! It makes no sense at all.' Osman nodded in agreement, but what could one say? It was true nevertheless.

'You've given Nik Mat jampi for his kite,' Maryam phrased her statement as a question. Omar nodded vaguely and applied himself to the cakes before him. Maryam reflected she'd already consumed a week's worth of snacks during the day, but accepted it philosophically. There was no other choice.

'How often?' Maryam pressed him after eating one, maybe two cakes (courtesy demanded it). Omar looked uncomfortable, and looked between Maryam and Osman as if deciding who might be more forgiving. Apparently neither, so he sighed and began.

'I helped him, yes. He was a professional flyer and I gave him all his jampi.' He said proudly. 'He had a new kite now, so I gave him even more to help him win with this new kite. What a kite! Have you seen it?' He looked enthusiastic, but then remembered why they were at this house and turned sombre again.

Maryam kept her expression composed and continued to look at him. 'Just kite magic? Not any other kind?'

Omar shrugged: 'Well, to help him and keep the others back, that's all. Nothing evil, if that's what you're asking.' He looked sharply at her. 'If you're thinking I offered him any black magic you're wrong. This is for kite flying. No one's supposed to get hurt during kite flying. It isn't that kind of thing.'

'But someone did,' Osman reminded him. 'What about Salim?'

Omar seemed to turn pale, and Maryam swore he actually looked worried just for an instant. He recovered quickly. 'Salim, yes, he's from Kampong Banggol. And, as you say, just started, but apparently talented. He was close behind Nik Man today at the contest. Ordinarily, I'd say he wouldn't have a chance, but he was holding his own. He actually won!'

'So we hear,' Maryam observed.

'Did you give Salim his jampi as well?' Maryam asked. Omar looked pleased and yet a bit worried. 'I gave him a few jampi. He was new, you know. Not a real contender, like Nik Man. I'd like to think I helped him.'

'Really?' said Maryam drily. 'And would Nik Man like to think the same?'

'No!' Omar assured her hurriedly. 'You know, I was Nik Man's official bomoh, though I know that sounds strange. But every professional flyer has a bomoh he works with all the time to keep the jampi on his kites all the time. And usually, well, all the time, you work with one flyer. But this ...' Omar looked thoughtful and perhaps a touch guilty.

'Nik Man has knowledge. He has jampi all the time; he doesn't need to get it every time he flies. He's a competitor.' He nodded.

'And all his knowledge is from you.' Osman stated.

Omar nodded slowly. 'But then Salim, he asked me ...' he hesitated. 'He can be difficult ...'

'You're afraid of him,' Maryam surmised. 'He asked you and you were afraid to say no. Did he threaten you?'

Omar blushed. 'I should have said no. You're right. But I was, am, a little afraid of his temper. And I only gave him a jampi or two, nothing major.'

'Did Nik Man know?'

Omar nodded sorrowfully. 'He heard Salim bragging after he'd won, and he thanked me for my jampi.' He put his hand on his forehead. 'That man could not keep his mouth shut!' he said bitterly. 'There was no reason to do that.'

'Was Nik Man angry?'

He nodded. 'I should have said no to Salim. I really should have.'

'Why didn't you'?

Omar sighed. 'I should have, I know.'

'I didn't ask you that,' Osman said testily.

Omar was taken aback, 'No, you're right. Why didn't I? I was scared. You know, Salim can be threatening.'

'You were greedy,' Maryam said flatly, picking up a small cake and examining it. 'You thought you'd make some extra money and no one would ever find out about it.'

Omar looked miserable. 'Maybe.'

'And maybe you'd have some more business on the side,' Maryam commented. 'But as I understand it, people want their bomoh to be loyal to them when it comes to kite jampi. Don't they? And if you have a reputation for helping other people who are competing against them, that would not be very good, would it?'

Omar seemed mesmerized by her speech, and sat silent. 'So,' she summed up, 'rather than helping you, I think Salim actually hurt you with his announcement, and he could hurt your business with Nik Mat and with other people who might think about using you. He did you no favours, did he?'

Omar didn't answer, so Maryam prodded him. 'Did he?'

'No,' he answered like a schoolboy. 'I don't think so.'

'And were you angry?' she continued, speaking softly.

'I ... I suppose so.'

'And did you kill him?'

Osman really thought he might answer 'yes' just to keep up the rhythm, but apparently this actually penetrated, and he drew back. 'No, I didn't,' he stated firmly. 'I didn't kill him.'

Chapter IV

Maryam thought of these as home visits, to see their suspects in their own environments. She realized she was likely to learn a great deal more about Kampong Banggol than she ever wanted to know, and would be spending more time there than anyone who didn't live there really should.

Nik Man and Sharifah lived in a neat, recently painted house, with contrasting carved trim, and flowerpots on each step up to the porch. A motorbike was parked beneath the house, and the yard was severely swept. There were several small children playing in front of the house, apparently deeply involved with mud, and several chickens wandering around them, but not too close, as these chickens must have already learned.

Maryam called from the bottom of the steps while Osman and Rahman stood quietly behind her, and Sharifah came out of the house to call them up. If she was uneasy about their visit she gave no sign, and invited them in with an untroubled smile. She was very pretty, with thick black hair cut in a bob, and large dark eyes. Her smile was bright and she laughed easily. 'Look at those mudskippers,' she motioned to the children below. 'Two of them are mine and the rest are neighbours. I think I'll have to wash them outside before I let them in!'

She ushered them into her living room and motioned to the couch, then went to call Nik Man, who came in looking as friendly as his wife. He greeted them as though he had hoped for nothing more from the day than that they would come to his house, and asked politely if they'd prefer hot or cold drinks.

'Cold, if it isn't any trouble,' Maryam asked.

'Of course,' Sharifah smiled and disappeared, and Maryam complemented him on his children. He laughed. 'The ones covered in mud?' Yes, we have two. Little ones, two boys. Hoping for a girl next,' he laughed again. Sharifah laughed with him as she returned with the drinks. They seemed like an extremely happy family, Maryam thought.

'Terrible thing,' she began, about Salim. They both regarded her levelly, and Maryam thought this might be the case with some of the most honest suspects she'd ever seen. No one so far had made much of a fuss with artificial sorrow about Salim. Strange, somehow, to be discussing someone's death where everyone, including the man's own wife, seemed completely calm about it.

'Mm, yes,' Sharifah said noncommittally. 'Yes, a shame.'

'You didn't like him much,' Maryam observed.

Sharifah and Nik Man exchanged a quick look. 'He was not an easy man to be around,' Nik Man began. 'Terrible temper, mean to his wives, always getting divorced. You know.'

'Any children?' Osman asked professionally.

'None.'

Maryam lifted her eyebrows. "Married several times …?'

Nik Man added, 'and no children. Yes, that's true. Though

his wife Halimah has children and grandchildren of her own.'

'He must have been disappointed.'

'I'm not sure,' Sharifah said, thoughtfully, 'I don't think he would have been a very good father, or that he was much interested in it. I don't see him paying that much attention to someone else, like you do when you have children. And then, his temper, which has only gotten worse.'

'Do you think there were people with a good reason to want to kill him?'

'Many,' Nik Man responded. 'He wasn't nice.'

'Like at the contest?'

'I'm not sure it would be worthwhile to kill him just because he won a single competition,' Nik Man answered calmly, with no hint of discomfort. 'He can certainly get people angry, though, carrying on and bragging as he did.'

'How about Omar giving him jampi?'

Now Nik Man flushed. 'That was wrong, if you ask me. I've been working with him for so long, and then to just give some to Salim like that. He owed me loyalty. I don't care if he says Salim threatened him. Omar knows how important loyalty is. He betrayed me!' He breathed deeply and sought to control himself. 'But anyway, Omar is fine and healthy.'

'Will you continue to use him?' Osman asked.

Nik Man shook his head, as Sharifah watched him anxiously. 'I don't think so. I'm going to look for someone else, someone trustworthy. I can't keep checking on my bomoh to make sure he's not working against me. It doesn't make any sense. Why have one then?'

'That's right!' Sharifah agreed. 'He's supposed to help you, not make you upset. There are other bomoh who do this kind of magic.' This had clearly been a subject for discussion.

'So then Omar's been a big loser here,' Rahman commented, jotting down something in his notebook.

Nik Man shrugged again. 'If it's something he cares about, which I'm not sure he does.'

'On another topic,' Maryam began, 'how long have you known Dris?'

'Oh, forever,' Nik Man answered. 'We're both born here, went to school together.'

'And he's worked with you since you were kids.'

He nodded. 'That's right.'

'Isn't it a little … odd, that he's still your helper? I thought most helpers were boys who were learning about kites.'

'Mostly.' He seemed unconcerned. 'But Dris, he never really wanted to fly a kite, and seemed happy to help out. And by now, you know, we're used to each other, so it's very easy.'

'He seems devoted,' Rahman commented.

'Yes, maybe,' Nik Man answered. Neither he nor Sharifah seemed particularly interested in the topic.

Maryam and the two policeman rose and made their farewells, walking slowly down the steps where they ran into a tall older woman, looking enough like Sharifah to be her older sister, who looked at them sternly.

'My sister, Bahiyah,' Sharifah called from the porch. 'Come up, Kakak! Get out of the sun!'

'You're investigating this murder,' Bahiyah informed them,

and they could but agree. She nodded. 'Looking for the murderer, are you?'

'Yes, of course,' Maryam answered politely. 'Do you have any information you think we ought to know?'

She snorted with derision. 'I certainly do. You should look closely at this Dris. A loafer. I don't trust him. Always hanging around here, looking at Sharifah, though Sharifah of course never notices him. Why would she? You look at him.' She turned from them and stomped up the stairs, leaving them staring open mouthed after her.

'What was that?' Maryam asked.

Chapter V

Dris intrigued her the most, with his boy's status and devotion to Nik Man. It seemed odd to her, and she believed whatever seemed odd was probably significant. She wondered, too, about his wife, and how she reacted to living with a man who subordinated himself to be the 'boy'.

She and Osman left the police car on the road and walked down the winding dirt paths into Kampong Banggol to find Dris' house. When they found it, his wife Latifah was sitting outside, folding laundry. She was a plain woman, with strong features, narrow eyes and a neat bun, dressed in a T-shirt and sarong. She'd clearly heard about them, and looked profoundly unimpressed, but waved them up onto the porch. Dris came out and, folding his sarong carefully around his legs, sat down and looked at Osman, not angrily, but not in a friendly way either.

'Would you like a cigarette?' Osman asked. Dris waved his hand; as the host, it was up to him to provide refreshments, at least at first, and they waited silently while Latifah prepared coffee and snacks. She served them in stony silence as well, giving Maryam a look of annoyance as she sat away from them on the porch and lit one of her own home-grown smokes.

Osman silently offered his pack of Rothmans and both lit up, absently watching the steam rise from the coffee cups. Osman settled back to be comfortable while listening to the story he knew would now unfold, hoping it would actually be the truth and not require him to sift through layers of deceit. Dris also weighed the possible benefits of truth versus fiction, and how likely a fiction might be detected. He wasn't sure about Osman, who was, after all, from the west coast and possibly therefore more gullible; Maryam, however, would be a different story altogether.

'It was the kites,' he said softly, 'that's what really started it. I mean, we were friends since we were kids, we grew up together, but of course, with families and kids and work, you don't have time to be together. Who does?' He shook his head. 'But we did, because I was his "coach" and we spent a lot of time together on the kites. He flew it, but we worked together.

'He needed my help. It's a lot to think about, flying. And it's always better to have someone else who takes care of things: the kites, the strings, keeping track of when you're flying. Like a manager, right? Kids do this when they're apprentices to flyers, but I just kept with it. I understood him, and he knew he could depend on me.

'Not everyone has a manager, but Nik Man knew he was lucky, and he would make sure to give me credit.' He smiled. 'He would say, "Dris here knows more about it than I do!" I was proud when I heard it. I knew he valued me.'

'You were inseparable.' Osman offered.

'No, you can't say that. We each had families, work, you know …'

'But you were willing to follow him.'

Dris looked uncomfortable, and lit another cigarette. From the sideways glances Dris now shot him, Osman believed he might be getting to the heart of the matter.

'I suppose that's true. We were friends, you know: *bagai kunyet dengan kapur:* like turmeric and lime.'

'Sharifah's older sister, she said we should talk to you. She said you were in love with Sharifah.'

'Did she?' Dris asked with a kind of objective interest.

They both sat silent. Osman finally asked, 'What does that mean?'

'She would think that,' Dris offered vaguely. 'But it wasn't true.' Osman simply waited, expecting a pro-forma denial. Dris smiled at him: an odd, triumphant smile. 'It wasn't Sharifah, no. It was Nik Man.'

Osman heard it, but for a moment did not understand it. He could not react at all, replaying the words in his head to see if he could make sense of it. Dris sat imperturbable, relieved to have it in the open. It was the first time he had said it in public, the first time he'd heard the words he said to himself out in the world, and he wanted to laugh with the lifting of his burden. There! It didn't seem nearly so bad now.

Maryam looked back to check on Latifah, who seemed oblivious, smoking a cigarette, leaning against the wall. 'So, Che Dris,' she said conversationally, 'Did Nik Man know about this? Did you tell him.'

Dris nodded silently, looking at the floor.

'What did he say?' she asked gently.

He was silent for a moment, then swallowed hard. 'Nothing

really. He looked at me, and never said anything. Like he didn't hear it.'

'Or didn't want to,' Maryam surmised. 'But you were still friends after that.'

'Yes. He never mentioned it, and so, well, I didn't either. Better not to, you see.'

'You're right,' Maryam agreed. 'If people don't react to hearing that, it's better not to say it again.' Dris looked amazed that he was having this conversation with Maryam, as though this were the most usual thing in the world, as if there were nothing wrong or detestable about what he'd told her. He had never imagined discussing this with anyone, particularly a respected mak cik with a police officer present.

'It must have upset you when he didn't react,' she continued.

Dris shrugged. 'I didn't really expect him to. I mean, maybe I hoped, you know, I guess you always hope if you say something like that, but no, I didn't really think he felt the same.' He sighed, and blinked back sudden tears. 'I didn't think he did, but I wanted him to.'

'Did it make you angry?' she asked softly.

'Angry?' He looked at her. 'Of course not. I mean, really, could I have thought he did? Did he say anything to make me think so? Had he promised me anything? Never!' He spoke more heatedly now. 'I would be angry maybe if I thought I'd been told something, or if I really thought he loved me and now he didn't, but I never thought that. Angry?' He repeated. 'Why would I be?'

'I just wondered,' she said, as though it didn't matter. 'People get angry about the strangest things.'

'Was he angry at you?' Osman asked, having recovered his wits. 'When you told him.'

Dris shook his head. 'Not angry at all. Surprised, maybe, but since he never said anything I don't really know.'

'Did your wife know? Did you tell her?'

Dris shook his head, then looked suddenly toward her, as though it had just occurred to him that Latifah might hear him. He looked frightened. 'Um. No, I didn't tell her.'

'Did she know?' Maryam prompted him.

'I knew.' Latifah rose suddenly, silently. She was still smoking the cigarette Maryam had seen in her hands. 'Of course I knew, even if he didn't tell me. I knew something for a long time.' She looked sadly at her husband. 'You're not a bad husband,' she told him, 'but there was something missing, always. I didn't really know why, until I realized you … .loved … Nik Man. Then I knew.' She sighed. 'But what is there to do? *Seperti parut di muka, puru di bibir*: like the scar on your face or the sore on your lip. There's nothing. The kids …' She trailed off and looked regretfully at her husband. 'Sad, isn't it?' She sat on the floor, joining the others, and lighting a new cigarette. Dris looked dumbfounded, as he had off and on throughout the visit.

'No one really thinks about these things, you know, or suspects them, unless it's just so obvious,' she said to Maryam. 'A boy who isn't acting like a *pondan,* who'd even give something like that a thought? I didn't, my parents didn't, even Dris' parents didn't. It took me a while after we were married to think he wasn't as interested as he should have been. I mean, we have children, but I knew he wasn't, he didn't, well, you know. I thought it was me, I mean me myself, not women, but then I began to realize how he looked around Nik Man and suddenly, it came to me. I couldn't believe it. I guess everyone would say that, but it's true. And I could tell Nik Man didn't see it at all, but then he wasn't looking for it. He was in love with his wife.'

Dris started as if to argue, but she waved him down. 'Don't tell me he didn't, or that you loved me. Either way, it's a lie. He did love Sharifah; they were really a perfect match. And you, well, you may like me and love your kids, but you certainly aren't in love with me.

'I thought about a divorce, of course,' she took a deep drag on her cigarette. 'But the kids, the money, I kept thinking maybe in a year or so, then another year, and another. If there were someone I wanted to go to, I would have gone. But there wasn't.' She looked sad. Maryam poured her a cup of tea and patted her shoulder.

'It must be awful for you.'

Latifah shrugged. 'Still better than having your husband come home with a second wife, or divorce you with no money. Or beat you, or drink, or gamble. I guess.' She smiled with no joy at all. 'I'm better off than some.'

Maryam agreed, but was still draining. Latifah appeared to be taking things very philosophically, but it had to rankle. 'Are you angry at Nik Man?'

'No, why? It isn't his fault. And besides,' she said, completely pragmatic, 'if not him, then maybe Dris would find someone else and it would be worse. You know, someone who would respond. Then it could be really bad. At least I know Nik Man wouldn't encourage him.'

Dris hung his head, hearing his wife outline things so coldly, so business-like. He'd had no idea she thought this way about him, or that she'd known. She'd never said anything about it, or given him any sign, or, he amended, given him any sign he'd actually noticed. He wished with all his heart he were different, that he had loved her and not someone else, but there was nothing he could do about it.

He looked at Osman and Maryam and saw pity on their faces: he didn't know whether it was for him or for Latifah, or maybe both. He was ashamed that things had come to this, that Salim was dead, and wondered if he had brought any of it on himself.

Chapter VI

'I didn't expect that,' Osman murmured to Maryam as they drove away. The rest of the interview had been awkward, their goodbyes hurried and no one met anyone else's eyes. Maryam took a deep breath and closed her eyes, offering a heartfelt prayer that Mamat had never shown any such proclivities, and she guessed it was too late now. Of course, as Latifah had so cogently pointed out, bringing home a second wife or chasing other women was no better; men and sex, Maryam thought sadly, were often a poisonous combination.

'Neither did I,' Maryam told him, 'but do you think it would make him kill Salim because he insulted Nik Man?

'I don't know whether he did it, but I do think it's a motive,' Osman ruminated. 'It seems such an … explosive situation. And you know, that kind of thing,' Osman blushed, discussing this so baldly with Maryam, 'it's illegal.'

'You aren't going to arrest him!'

'No, of course I'm not,' Osman hurriedly assured her. 'Azrina would never allow it.'

Maryam smiled. Osman's wife had already made clear she believed justice should be generously sprinkled with mercy, and she expected her husband to follow this precept. 'But what I mean is, could Salim have noticed, have threatened him with that? Or could someone else have done it? It seems a great opportunity for blackmail, though I don't know what Dris could come up with. He's not a rich man.'

Maryam could not think of an answer.

* * *

Aliza, Maryam's younger daughter, had as usual taken charge of the family, herding her younger brother Yi to the table and laying out the *ayam percik* she had picked up on the market on her way home. Aliza was almost finished now with Teacher's College in Kota Bharu, and in only a few months would be teaching her own classes at the local elementary school and ruling over her own students.

It was while they weren't looking, Maryam felt, that Aliza had suddenly turned into a beauty, indeed, as striking as her older sister Ashikin, who was widely acknowledged to be one of the prettiest girls in Kelantan, and had been so since babyhood. While Ashikin had never gone through an ungainly period, Aliza had to grow into her beauty, and did so without anyone noticing until her transformation was complete.

The first to really see it was her now fiancé, Rahman, a police hero who adored her. Maryam and Rubiah had been present at their first meeting, and saw Rahman succumb to the thunderbolt. They were amused by it at first, though they both believed it would lead to a serious offer, and as usual, they were right.

Soon after he had initially been felled, his parents called on

Maryam and Mamat to ask, obliquely, for her hand. Aliza told them to accept the offer, after the requisite jockeying. She liked Rahman, and had heard the stories of his heroism, and therefore could admire him, something she found difficult to do with many men. Like her sister and mother before her, she knew what she wanted when she saw it, and took immediate charge to see things went as she decided.

Their wedding was scheduled for soon after her graduation, but Aliza was hardly the model of an intemperate bride, and remained quite unfazed by the whole process. Maryam believed she'd be as calmly in control of her marriage as she was of her family and her students – a daughter she could be proud of, and a future pillar of her own family. She was content she'd done her job as a mother well.

Aliza was interested in her mother's work, and quietly believed she was the perfect heir to the business. She sat quietly next to her mother and her mother's cousin Rubiah as Maryam explained to her cousin all that had happened.

Rubiah was silent after hearing it all, looking troubled. 'I feel I should say "poor man", killed like that,' she said at last. 'But "poor man" doesn't seem to describe him at all. From what I'm hearing, most people hated him, and any one of the people you've talked to had at least an adequate reason to kill him.

'Does this thing between Dris and Nik Man really have anything to do with it? It's completely unexpected, so it seems important, but is it? Maybe it's keeping our attention away from the real reason. I mean,' she explained slowly, 'you know, it seems like blackmail could be a reason for killing him, if he was trying that. But it might also be a dead end, and there's another reason we haven't seen yet because this looks so ... strange. Right? It could have to do with Dris or his wife, or Nik Man or his, but maybe it has nothing to do with them, even though it seems as if that could easily lead to murder.'

Maryam looked at her with pride and affection. 'You're right!' she cried happily. 'I knew you'd see something I missed.'

Rubiah graciously accepted the encomium, although she was somewhat surprised by it. Maryam did not hand out credit lightly.

'Besides,' she continued, riding her wave of approbation, 'you really only heard Dris' story. There's nothing else to confirm it, and while I'm not saying he's lying (why lie about that after you've told the truth about something far more serious?), we'd still need to have more than just his word. Or Latifah's for that matter.' She nodded at Maryam.

'True,' Maryam agreed. Aliza looked wide-eyed at them both, and Rubiah turned to her and said casually, 'How's the wedding planning?'

Aliza shrugged and looked bored. 'Oh, it's fine. Ashikin is doing a lot of the work.' She acknowledged Rubiah's raised eyebrow and Maryam sighed. 'She knows so much more about it! And Rosnah is helping and they love weddings. I have school,' she said defensively, and Rubiah laughed.

'And if you didn't? Would that matter?'

'Probably not,' Aliza admitted with good humour. 'I find this so much more interesting,' she said hopefully. 'And I'm an adult now, not like before,' when she'd been so badly hurt in the course of one of her mother's investigations. 'I can help, you know'.

Maryam looked doubtful, afraid to forbid it lest it push Aliza into some precipitous and possibly dangerous action, but afraid to agree lest it do the same. Aliza reminded her so much of herself at her age, though by then Maryam had been married with a small child. Well, Aliza was going to teacher training college, wasn't she? And how proud she was of that!

'We'll see,' she temporized, thinking it might not be a bad thing to have Aliza's help, though of necessity it would lead her to see and hear things perhaps not proper for a young girl. Though kids grew up faster these days and Aliza was not one to miss anything going on around her. 'We'll see.'

Chapter VII

Rahman was leaning on his car in front of Sultanah Zainab Teacher Training College at the end of the school day. When he saw Aliza skip down the front steps, unaware of him, he felt breathless, almost the same way he'd felt when he first saw her on the porch of her house. She was so pretty, so confident, and when she saw him and smiled, he beamed back at her with unalloyed joy. He always felt lucky when he saw her, to think that she was actually his fiancée and that he was going to marry her.

Rahman was second in command to Osman, and his unofficial translator for Kelantanese. He'd been badly hurt several years earlier running down a suspect in Kota Bharu's crowded market, but he'd gotten his man and his courage and strength deeply impressed everyone who'd witnessed it. His head wound left him hospitalized and unresponsive, and very nearly despaired of, though not by his close family, who clustered around him and urged him to return to them. He did, which his mother attributed to her own force of personality, because her son would be afraid to die without her permission, which was certainly not forthcoming. So in fact, he recovered because he had no choice, and his mother was particularly proud of her part in it. And when, as proof (if more were necessary) of his complete recovery, he asked his parents to sue for Aliza's hand, her happiness was complete.

Aliza would be a wife in the mould of both his mother and hers: strong and competent, with no kittenish avowals of helplessness. Rahman knew she'd be his equal, if not his superior, and he welcomed it, being both a well-brought-up Kelantanese boy and a modern man of the world. Besides, he had no choice.

'My mother's on another case,' she told him when they sat in his air-conditioned car. Aliza thought it might be nice to have air conditioning in her own home, when the time came, though the details of cooling a kampong house, built to stay open to any cooling breeze, were rather daunting. 'Do you know what it's about?'

Rahman nodded, having heard from Osman about the kite corpse, as he called it. 'Someone was killed in a kite flying contest,' he told her. Though he planned to spare her the graphic details, lest it upset her, he soon found that he revealed it all under her skilful yet affectionate interrogation, and then wondered how it had all come out.

'Hung by a kite string,' Aliza mused. 'Someone must have really hated him.'

'Why would they hate him more than killing him any other way?'

'I suppose you're right,' she conceded, considering. 'But this seems rougher, somehow. You know, the glass on the string, hanging him from a tree like that. The killer must have been furious, for some reason. It doesn't sound planned.' She looked at him. 'I don't know why,' she forestalled the next question, 'it just does. Like, he saw the string and the tree and suddenly said to

59

himself, "That's it. I'm killing him." I think, anyway. Or maybe a woman: his wife was angry with him.' She already knew the most familiar trope in Kelantanese life. 'Did he take another wife?'

'No, nothing like that. Though his wife wanted a divorce. I believe he may have hit her.'

Aliza made a sound of disapproval. 'Did she kill him?'

'We don't know for sure yet. It would take some strength to hang him like that, so I think we may first look for a man.'

Aliza thought. 'What else was there? Did he owe someone money? Steal their land? Kill their *kerbau*?'

He shrugged. 'Nothing I heard about.' He wished there was something he could offer her, he felt as if he hadn't been paying attention.

'Come in,' she urged him as they arrived in Kampong Penambang. Mamat waved to them from the porch where he was feeding his songbirds. Rahman sat down to admire them while Aliza prepared some coffee and cakes for them as they leaned comfortably back against the wall of the house. Mamat was quite fond of his son-in-law-to-be, and was pleased to see how much Rahman cared for Aliza. Of course, who wouldn't? He was very proud of his children.

Gangly Yi joined them, not daring to ask for a cigarette which his father wouldn't allow, but which Yi saw as an emblem of manhood, and yearned to try. He had attempted it with his friends at school, but it had been in secret and unsatisfactory, since its very secrecy destroyed it symbolism. Soon, Yi thought; if not his father, surely Rahman might be prevailed upon to give him one. If Aliza didn't find out.

Chapter VIII

Aliza had discussed the case with her mother, driven by her concern there was no adequate motive. 'No one knows anything,' she announced while picking through a selection of Rubiah's cakes. Maryam tried to remember whether at the age of 18 she herself could eat limitlessly and still be so slim; it seems she might have been able to, though her willowy days were clearly behind her now. If her metabolism had slowed, she was at least more confident in herself and so could continue eating cakes anyway – it was one of the few advantages of middle age and grandmotherhood.

'I don't know about that,' she said mildly. 'He was killed at the contest; it seems to me we have three suspects, all of whom disliked him, all of whom were there. We just have to pick one – the one who did it, I mean,' she hastily amended, lest Aliza think she chose the guilty by herself.

'Could there have been other people at the contest who hated him also?'

'It seems there were people who hated him everywhere,' Maryam observed. 'What a way to go through life. But right now I think we should concentrate on our most likely people. None of them seemed the least bit upset to see him gone.'

'Can you imagine being married to him and feeling that way?' Aliza asked. As could be expected, the topic of being married was much on her mind lately. 'It must be awful. Do you think they'd be getting divorced if he were alive?'

'I don't doubt it for a moment,' her mother told her. 'I think his wife had had just about enough of him. The question to me is why she stayed with him after they were divorced twice. She told us, remember, that they were already divorced with two talak. So I was wondering, why not just leave? You don't want to be with him, and she seemed to me a pretty competent person, don't you think?'

Aliza agreed. 'I don't think she was staying because she couldn't figure out how to eat if she wasn't with him. Honestly, I don't understand that kind of thinking at all.' She stopped herself. 'Anyway, that's not what I wanted to talk about now. I think you're right. It's odd she would stay. She knew what he was like. I think,' she announced, 'we need to talk to her again. Whenever there's something you can't understand, it's probably part of the solution,' she quoted her mother, who couldn't bear having things around her which made no sense.

Maryam was amused by her daughter and wondered if it had been genetically determined they would be so alike.

Maryam, Rubiah and Aliza went to speak to Halimah, Salim's widow, but when they arrived at her porch, no one was home. A helpful neighbour came over when she saw them calling, to tell them Halimah was not at home, but had gone to see her daughter, in nearby Kampong Cabang Tiga.

'Sad about the husband, isn't it?' the neighbour began. 'How do you know Che Halimah?'

'We're helping the police,' Maryam told her, trying to keep her tone neutral, so as not to come off as too bossy, or too proud.

'Ah,' said the woman, 'you're the detectives from Kampong Penambang. I've heard of you! So,' she sat down on the steps of Halimah's empty house, 'you're investigating Salim's death, is it? Very suspicious.'

'Really?' asked Rubiah.

The woman snorted in derision. 'Really?' she mimicked. 'Well, he was murdered, wasn't he? He didn't hang himself with a kite string. And besides,' she leaned forward, 'who will miss him? No one. He was a terrible person, an annoyance to everyone who dealt with him.'

'Even just neighbours,' Aliza asked.

'Yes! If you can believe it. Always picking fights with everyone. He has some rice land over there,' she waved her hand vaguely indicating inland, beyond the coconut palms, 'and he's argued with every single person whose land borders on his, *and* everyone whose land he even has to pass through to get to it. Can you imagine?'

Maryam also leaned forward. 'There are people like that, I know. *Rambut sama hitam, hati masing-masing:* we all have black hair, but each has his own heart. But tell me, why would someone like Halimah stay married to him? Even, as I hear, after two talak?'

'That's the question,' the woman lit up a cigarette, clearly pleased to have found a reason to take a break from the laundry she'd been doing. 'I don't understand it myself. You know, Cik

Halimah has a little stall at the market over in Cabang Tiga, and has her daughter and two sons, so she doesn't need a place to live or someone to feed her. And she has no children with Salim, so why stay? And they fought a lot, though I tell you it was Salim's fault, not hers. She's nice, friendly, good businesswoman' this was a most important quality, 'and she didn't need him. Everyone likes her, no one liked him. So why?'

'He was married before, wasn't he?'

'Yes, he had a few wives I think, I can't remember, but it never lasted all that long because he'd start fighting with them and they'd decide they didn't like him. No children with any of them, so really no reason to stay. I think they all married other people and settled down. Cik Halimah married him after her children were grown, so that wasn't part of it. I think,' she lowered her voice, 'he tried to hit her a couple times, but she wouldn't stand for it. I saw him once standing on the porch right here with blood trickling down his neck from where she hit him with a *parang*. Not to kill him, of course,' she added quickly, 'she didn't stab him but she hit him with it when he tried to hit her. Good for her!' she said with feeling.

They all agreed. 'It makes even less sense now after what you've told me,' Rubiah mused. 'They've already been divorced twice, it seems to me it was all taken care of, so why go back?'

The woman shook her head and took a drag of her cigarette. 'That's the real mystery if you ask me. I can think of a million reasons to kill him, but I can't think of any to marry him.'

Chapter IX

They hailed a bicycle-driven taxi to go to Cabang Tiga – it was already afternoon and too hot to walk in the sun. It wasn't too long a ride, but both Maryam and Rubiah wanted to arrive refreshed and alert, not exhausted by the heat, which was already shimmering off the tar on the main road and making the air itself feel heavy.

They quickly found Halimah's daughter's house: a rambling kampong house with several children running in and out of it, and a well in the front yard. Halimah had the place of honour in the shade of the porch, her back against the wall, and a cup of coffee in front of her. Next to her sat what was clearly her daughter, who looked much like her: nicely plump with a long face, arched eyebrows and lively black eyes. Both smiled as they saw the three women approach the house.

'Cik Maryam, Cik Rubiah, welcome! Come up out of the sun and have a drink,' Halimah called light-heartedly. 'Maimun, meet Cik Maryam and Cik Rubiah', she said to her daughter, 'these are the detectives I told you about. They work with the police.' They ascended the stairs and sat, with smiles all around. 'And who is this?' Halimah asked of Aliza. 'Are you helping detect as well?'

'My daughter, Aliza,' Maryam told her. 'She's studying

to be a teacher.'

'Very nice,' said Maimun, 'welcome. Let me fetch some coffee,' and she rose.

Halimah treated this as a pleasant social call; Maryam could find no sign of nervousness or reluctance in her manner. She asked Aliza if she was working, heard she was engaged to a police officer and planned to be married soon, that her sister was expecting another baby, as was her brother, his first, and that her little brother was a bit of a pest but they hoped he'd soon grow out of it.

Halimah beamed at Maryam. 'I see I must congratulate you on all these things happening in your family. So nice to hear good news, I must say. I'm sick of hearing about tragedies.'

Maimun had returned with coffee and cigarettes and curry puffs, hot and fresh, and Rubiah protested. 'You must be making these for dinner, we couldn't possibly eat them now. You're going to so much trouble for us, and there is no need to.'

Maimun smiled at them. 'I'd be hurt if you didn't eat them. I didn't know you were coming but I must have sensed it, and made these for you.'

Both Maimun and her mother were so welcoming, polite and happy Maryam was ashamed she was actually asking them about a murder. She prayed fervently that Halimah would have nothing to do with it. She would hate to see this woman whom she liked, and who spoke to her so nicely, have to be punished for the death of someone who sounded so insufferable. Not very professional, she admitted, but true.

After a bit of chitchat, Maryam began, 'I hate to ask you

these things, Cik Halimah, when we are all having such a good time here, and you have both been so kind, but I'm afraid I must.'

'Of course you must,' Halimah agreed with her. 'I knew that's why you were here. Don't worry, you can ask whatever you'd like.'

When, in the long and sorry history of murder, had a killer ever invited someone to interrogate them like this? She could not really have done it, Maryam thought, and then tried to put the thought out of her mind because as a detective helping the Kota Bharu Police Department, it was a very unprofessional thought.

'When was the funeral?' Rubiah asked quietly.

'Oh, yesterday,' Halimah said, lighting a cigarette and offering them around to everyone but Aliza. It wouldn't be right for Aliza to start before marriage. 'Not too big: the neighbours, of course, and Salim's brother from Pasir Mas. His family isn't too big, and his other brother lives in Kuala Lumpur and couldn't make it back.' They all digested this bit of brotherly abandonment – couldn't make it back for your brother's funeral? Unheard of.

'I know what you're thinking,' Halimah informed them, 'what's happening between the brothers that he wouldn't come back? A fight years ago, you know, Salim and his brother aren't that much different. Both difficult. So you can imagine what kind of relationship they had! Anyway, I'm glad the funeral's over. This whole thing is so tiring.'

Aliza was surprised to hear someone describe their husband's murder in such mundane terms, but told herself that this was the fruit of many years of irascibility, and that it should be a lesson in making sure you were at least decent to people.

'It sounds bad, doesn't it? What I just said. It is bad.' Halimah didn't seem too upset by her confession.

Maryam nodded, though at what in particular she could not have said. 'May I ask a personal question?'

'Isn't that what you're here for?'

'Well, yes. You see, Cik Halimah, you seem such a nice person, a capable person, with children and grandchildren,' Maryam paused, uncertain how to go forward without giving offense.

'Why did she marry Salim? And why stay with him?' Maimun piped up. 'We all wondered that ourselves. Mak?'

'Alamak! Even I wonder about it, and I don't have a great reason to give you. He wasn't so bad when I married him, and I was kind of lonely. My husband had died,' she lowered her head for a moment, as did her daughter, 'and I didn't want to live alone.' She held up her hand as her daughter started to speak. 'I know I could live here but it isn't the same. Anyway, Salim was really nice at first – he could be when he wanted to – it's just that he didn't want to very often. That was his problem.

'So I married him. And I found out, as the months went by, how horrible he could be to live with. I kind of ignored it for a while, but then I was fed up. Completely. And we got one talak, a divorce. After that, he came back, promising to be nicer, to be a better husband, you know, all the promises they make when they want you to come home. So I tried again, and it didn't work this time either.

'He only wanted me back to cook for him, or to do something else for him. He was so selfish,' she continued with asperity, 'it was always what he wanted. Didn't even notice the kids at all.'

'I didn't like him coming here,' Maimun interrupted, 'though honestly, he wasn't interested in it. Mak came here by herself and that was fine with all of us. You never even talked about him as though you liked him,' she reminded her mother. 'I just don't get it.'

They all looked at Halimah waiting for an explanation. For the first time since she'd spoken to her, Maryam thought Halimah looked a little uncomfortable. 'I don't know,' she said shortly, but Maryam didn't believe it.

'Cik Halimah,' she said softly, 'I think there's something else.'

There was silence on the porch, during which Maryam could clearly hear the sounds of the children playing in the yard, of chickens scratching and clucking to each other beneath the house and the rattle of the cup as Aliza took a sip of coffee.

'Well,' Maryam prodded her gently. 'Is there something else?'

'I was waiting for my rice land,' she sighed. She looked around to all of them, but comprehension was not dawning yet. 'You know, when I first married him, he promised me his rice land in Kubang Kerian. It's good land, and it's big. You could rent it out to two different people if you wanted to.' She seemed to cheer up a little after her discomfort, discussing the land she'd clearly spent a lot of time thinking about. 'I'm not saying it's the only reason I married him, but it was a part of it.' From the look on her daughter's face, Maryam surmised it had just occurred to her how big a part it was.

'He farmed that land himself, but it was really too much for him. Besides, he wasn't that hardworking, if you know what I mean.' They all knew what she meant. 'That land, which he promised me, would support not just me, but help my kids as well. And anyway,' she repeated, 'he promised it to me. It was mine.'

'Who else wanted it?'

'I don't know. His nephew and nieces? Maybe they did, but they never came to see him: they didn't like him much, so I don't see how they could be counting on him leaving them something.'

'You'd be surprised what people count on with very little encouragement,' Rubiah commented.

'That's so,' agreed Halimah, now back to her own relaxed self since the secret was out. 'You're right about that, and nothing starts a family battle more easily than land inheritance, right? I know. But still, I earned it.' They all agreed with that, and Halimah's daughter looked unhappy,

'You didn't need to sell yourself to get rice land for us to inherit,' she said to her mother, as though no one else was listening. 'Mak, why didn't you tell me? I'd have told you to leave him and never mind what he promised you.'

'Is that why you went back to him after each talak?' Maryam asked, and Halimah nodded.

'He held it in front of me. And I'd put the time in – doesn't that sound terrible?' she mused. 'Now that I'm listening to it being said. Well,' she continued briskly, anxious to get the topic out of the way, 'it's done. What I mean to say is, I did it, I stayed for the land, and now I have it.'

'He signed it over last month, finally. And before you ask,' she lit another cigarette, 'I was going to get a divorce now that I had it. This would make it three talak and I think we'd be done.'

She looked relieved, having gotten this difficult story told and done with.

'I'm not saying I'm proud of it, you understand,' she said to Maryam and Rubiah, her contemporaries and therefore perhaps most likely to appreciate what she'd gone through and why. 'It wasn't a nice thing to do, and he wasn't a nice person. And if I'm honest, I must say listening to myself explain it I don't seem like such a nice person anymore either.'

'Mak!' her daughter cried. 'Don't say that!'

'It's probably true, but now that whole episode is over and I can go back to being someone I'm proud to be. I'm going to stay in the house, and I'm looking into renting out the land for the next planting season, which is less than a month away. I've had a lot of people asking about it so I shouldn't have any trouble.' She seemed satisfied with that. 'And I have my little stall in the Cabang Tiga market, so I should be just fine. And my kids will be that much better off.'

Maryam hated to say it, but had to. 'So really, you didn't need him anymore, now that the land's signed over to you.'

She snorted, 'I never needed him. I just wanted what he promised me. But that's why I wanted a divorce now. I'd spent enough time with him. I was through.'

'Through enough to kill him?'

She sighed. 'I knew you were going to ask me that.'

Chapter X

It was just after dawn, and the household first began stirring. Maryam had just finished her Fajr prayer. She smoothed her hair and headed into the kitchen to prepare breakfast and lunches. She was slicing vegetables for *nasi lemak* when she heard a commotion on the porch, where Mamat's prize singing zebra doves, *merbok,* were kept in their fancy cages. Mamat's first task of the day was to feed them, often by hand, and to coo over them and fuss with the placement of the cages: neither too much sun nor too much shade. She headed out to see what the problem might be and was greeted by Mamat with a face as deadly pale as a corpse.

She cried out, appalled to see him, steadying herself against the door frame. Mamat pointed to a dove hanging from a beam by a glass encrusted kite string. The small, feathered body was swinging gently as Mamat cut it down; he began to cry. 'My merbok,' he sobbed, 'my little bird. Who would do this.' He cradled the bird and sank to his knees, his other doves cooing and fluttering in distress.

'Did you, did you see anyone?' Maryam stammered. This seemed more of an obscenity than killing a person, since what could that small beautiful bird have possibly done to deserve it?

Mamat was beside himself with grief, a grief he would never have shown in public even for the death of a family member. He bent over his dove, keening. Maryam was terrified.

'Mamat,' she pressed him. 'Did you see anything? Did you hear anything?'

He shook his head, not looking up. 'Nothing, nothing,' he cried. 'Who would kill my birds?'

Aliza, hearing the noise, stumbled out sleepily onto the porch, and then stopped and froze. She had never seen their father like this; she had never seen any adult like this, and few children. She turned wide-eyed stares at their mother, seeking an explanation.

'Your father's, I mean, our doves, they have been … attacked,' Maryam said, unable to really gather her thoughts. 'I don't know why.'

'The merbok was hung?' Aliza asked, astonished. 'Hung?'

'Yes, I think so. It looks like it.'

Aliza looked pale and frightened, but fought for composure. 'Mak, it's a warning for us. The murderer, he's telling us they know where we are.' Maryam stared at her. 'You know it's true,' she insisted. 'Why else would anyone kill a little bird, and such a terrible way to do it? Just like Salim: hung with a kite string.'

Maryam nodded mechanically. Of course, Aliza was correct. Nothing else made any sense. 'Go for the police,' she ordered her, and tried to coax Mamat back into the house.

* * *

Rahman looked alarmed. 'No one heard anything?' he asked yet again, hoping for another answer this time but none was forthcoming.

'Nothing,' Mamat repeated, 'I just came out here and there she was, hanging, poor thing.' He'd calmed down now, the presence of other people forcing him to be more controlled. His eyes were red and swollen, his face still pale, but both Osman and Rahman politely didn't notice it at all, and kept their eyes on Maryam and Aliza. Yi came out of the house, still sleep befuddled, and sat next to Aliza, yawning.

'What kind of person would do this?' Maryam demanded. 'Which one of the possible murderers we've been talking to would stoop to this?'

'Well, if they're already murderers,' Rahman began explaining, but a look from Aliza cut him short.

Mamat silently and hopelessly passed out cigarettes, and waved his hand over the coffee and cakes on the table. Maryam took her cigarette and looked absently at the ceiling, deep in thought.

'A kite flyer,' Osman answered Maryam. 'Someone who has the material, and who knows how to coat the string.'

'That's everyone,' Rubiah answered. 'Don't they all have those strings in their houses?'

Osman thought about it for a moment. 'You're right,' he told Rubiah. But this is evil, torturing such a sweet little bird. It's not just having the string, you know, it's having the mind that could think of something like this. A mind I just don't like.'

'It still could be anyone,' Rubiah responded. 'Any one of them could have a mind you just don't like, and one of them certainly does.'

Chapter XI

While Maryam would never publicly admit it, she often dreamt of her time as a tiger, as she remembered it, although she acknowledged, gratefully even, that this was an impossibility, a delusion, an illness. Nothing she'd known or seen during her life led her to think that were-tigers were real, or even more to the point, that she was herself one of them. And yet ...

Since that time, she slept either dreamlessly (the best option) or had vivid experiences as a tiger. These dreams were special, and she always woke with a mixture of exhilaration (from her experience as a tiger, in which she always lived in a state of heightened perception and a soaring feeling of power) and dread (this nightmare could begin again). She mentioned it to no one, and acknowledged it to herself only when forced. Usually, upon waking, she forced it to the back of her mind and willed herself to forget. Never again would she awake filthy and debris-covered, a disgrace to herself and her family.

But she knew the episode was not yet over, and feared a return. Now, as she once again threw herself into an investigation, she wondered whether her increased tiger self could more clearly see what had happened, could see or hear or smell things her human self did not even know existed. To be found again as a tiger, or even as an ex-tiger cleaning herself up would end her family. Mamat could never stand for it, and she suspected even her children would abandon her. It could not be risked for any reason.

When she had these dreams, she was troubled as she had never been before, thinking her life, and the people she loved, were available to her only if she kept her secret, and perhaps because of that were never hers to begin with. The bedrock of her existence had slid under her, leaving her ostensibly unwounded to the eyes of others, but she feared the loss of it all if anyone were to learn the truth, even if that truth was limited to her dreams.

* * *

At the police station, Maryam and Rubiah took up their positions in the official interrogation room, to better sift through the evidence they'd so far found, which was actually pitifully little. They were wearing down with what they believed was a lack of progress. Primed with curry puffs and sweet coffee, cigarettes and a sampler of Rubiah's cakes, the table was covered more with snacks than with paper, but that's they way they preferred to work.

Rubiah eyed Maryam as she picked through the cake assortment, seeming to focus entirely on which sort she would eat. She much preferred *onde-onde,* small rice flour balls covered with coconut flakes with a palm sugar centre. Rubiah had provided a good percentage of them in the platter before them, and yet was becoming increasingly annoyed watching her cousin choose so carefully.

'We're here to work on this case,' she said between her teeth when she could no longer control herself. 'Yam, all you're doing is choosing cakes.'

Rubiah thought Maryam would snap back at her, and was therefore surprised when she turned mildly to her and said, 'I can do both, you know. I find choosing cakes clears my mind to solve problems.' She gave Rubiah an understanding smile that made Rubiah grit her teeth all the harder, but she refused to be goaded. Maryam could so easily get the better of her, it was quite infuriating.

Osman appeared not to notice any of this, piling his own plate with the *tahi itek* cakes he preferred, frowning slightly as he stirred his coffee. Rubiah could not explain why this current charade of food arrangement was annoying her so, it was no different than what happened hundreds of times a day all over Kelantan. But she felt now that things were becoming more serious, though why she had to explain this to Maryam, whose home had been so meanly attacked, she could not understand. Maryam should have been whipping them all forward to find out who did this instead of weighing the choice of one cake over another, or whether or not to have another cigarette. Rubiah breathed deeply through her nose in an effort to calm herself and not to burst out in an unforgiveable breach of etiquette.

After what felt like an interminable summing up of all they knew, Osman continued on to outline his thinking. 'All the people I suspect are decent people with understandable motives. I'm not saying I would condone it, I'm not saying that. But at least I can figure out why any of them would have done it.' He looked morose.

'Can you figure out why anyone would have killed the bird?' Maryam asked.

He looked uncomfortable. 'No, that baffles me. Killing Salim could make sense. Killing a dove? None at all.'

'Is it possible it's someone else, who you haven't considered yet?' Rubiah asked quietly.

'It has to be someone who was there at the contest,' Osman told her.

'There were other people there,' she pointed out. 'Maybe one of them also had a reason. I mean, it could have been someone we don't even know about who was hiding in the bushes.'

Maryam prayed this was not the case, as the thought of finding everyone at the contest, let alone interviewing them, pre-emptively exhausted her. Thankfully, rounding them all up would not be her job, and for that she was deeply grateful.

'Yes, Man, maybe we should try to see everyone who was there, not just those three. We may find someone else who at least saw something.' She smiled encouragingly at Rubiah, sternly reminding herself that a crime investigation was nothing to get lazy about. One had to persevere.

Osman nodded and said, 'I should have done that earlier. I was so sure it was one of these three ...'

'And it still may be,' Maryam assured him. 'Don't decide they're innocent just yet.'

Starting with Nik Man, whom Osman reasoned would be the most likely person to know the majority of competitors and their supporters, Rahman and Zul, a junior policeman new to the force, painstakingly began to compile a list of everyone who was competing that morning. It seemed a relatively tight group, and working one at a time they managed to find out who had accompanied them to the contest, and find them as well. It was a good-sized crowd.

Nik Man and his wife Sharifah sat politely with Rahman to provide a list of contestants. Rahman wondered whether they were becoming impatient with them, and their endless questions, but both remained unflappable. Nik Man sat with his head back, envisioning the contest and trying to see who'd been there. It was a fairly comprehensive list, with about fifteen men competing. As for their supporters, Nik Man shook his head, it was hopeless for him to try to remember such a large crowd. Wouldn't it be better, he suggested, if Rahman asked each competitor who'd been there with him, and try to track it that way?

Looking at his list, Rahman asked, 'Which one of these people would have a reason to hate Salim, hate him enough to kill him?'

Nik Man laughed. 'All of them were probably fed up with him. But would that be enough to kill someone? I don't know, but you deal with this kind of thing all the time. Maybe you'll be able to find the secret.'

Rahman looked unhappily at his notebook, unwilling to tell Nik Man that he didn't deal with this kind of thing everyday – in fact, hardly at all. But he thought better of destroying Nik Man's faith in the Kota Bharu Police Department, of which he was a proud member. Better he overestimated Rahman's expertise than had no confidence in it whatsoever, though sadly, that was the state of mind in which Rahman found himself.

'Thank you,' he said as confidently as he could, trying to banish the doubt from his tone and assure them that the police were all over this. 'I'll be talking to these people and hopefully, we'll get this wrapped up right away.' He realized as soon as he said it that he was talking to one of his prime suspects, who might not share his desire to solve the case as quickly as possible, but the words were out and he could hardly take them back without verbally tripping all over himself. He said his goodbyes and gratefully left, safely sitting in the car where he could make no more verbal gaffes.

They worked their way down the list, visiting each of the contestants, taking names of their helpers, or their wives, or their friends who had come to cheer them on. None of them pretended to be upset about Salim's death: most simply shrugged, it having nothing to do with them, and although they didn't like Salim, they didn't hate him with burning passion either. Most simply thought that sooner rather than later he'd get bored with kite flying as he had with so many other hobbies and blessedly disappear from their contests. That he was permanently withdrawn from the fraternity of kite flying enthusiasts didn't appear to trouble them much.

While Rahman trudged through his list, Maryam and Rubiah returned to see Nik Man. He greeted them with his usual politeness dialled down several notches.

'I just spoke to the police,' he told them with a hint of impatience. 'I gave them all the names I knew.' He left unspoken, 'I have other things to do and now you're back again!' Nevertheless, he invited them up, provided a drink and sat back with an air of martyred resignation that Maryam could actually commiserate with. Unless he was actually the killer, of course, in which case she had no sympathy.

'It's just this,' she began, looking around to see if Sharifah was within earshot. 'I spoke to Dris,' and she paused.

Nik Man looked at her with now ill-concealed impatience. 'Yes, Mak Cik. You spoke to him. I know.'

'Did you know ... he's in love with you?'

'What?' He appeared floored, though Maryam wasn't sure she could trust it.

'Yes, he told me that.'

'He told you?'

Now it was Maryam's turn to be impatient. 'Yes. He told me, that's what I said.'

Nik Man sat back in his chair and stared. 'I, I ... I don't know what to say.'

'Have you heard it before?'

Nik Man looked confused. Maryam couldn't tell whether it was because he was shocked, or because he couldn't believe Dris would actually talk about it.

'Nik Man, I asked a very simple question. Had he spoken to you about it? Ever?'

Nik Man struggled with an answer. 'Well, I mean, well ...'

Maryam watched him flounder. He cleared his throat. 'I've know him since we were kids.' She nodded. 'It's just I didn't expect ...'

'Expect what?'

'To be talking about something like that.' Now, he too turned to look to see if his wife was near. 'He may have ... mentioned ... said, maybe, something about ...' He stopped speaking, but sat with an expression which reminded Maryam of a landed fish.

'He told you, then.'

Nik Man blushed. 'He may have said something.'

'Did he, or not?'

Nik Man looked frightened. 'He said it. I didn't.'

'We aren't here to look into that, you know. Just a murder. But I want to know what your relationship is with Dris. Is it just kite flying, or is it more?'

Nik Man didn't know where to look. 'We are just old friends who've known each other since childhood. And you know we work together on kites. There's no more to that. I'm married. So is he.'

'It doesn't seem to affect his feelings,' Maryam said gently. 'Married or not, we need to know what you are to each other.'

'Nothing. We're nothing to each other.'

'Surely friends and co-workers,' Rubiah corrected him. But Nik Man now seemed hell-bent on distancing himself from Dris. 'Just that. Nothing more. I have a wife, children. Do you think I would ever ...?'

'I don't know, and really, I'm not concerned except as to how it might lead someone to kill. For example,' she leaned toward him, 'might Dris have killed Salim for beating you at the contest? To protect you, as he would see it? To make you grateful to him?'

'I don't know about anything like that,' he mumbled. 'He never said anything to me about that.'

'Really?' said Rubiah kindly. 'I think maybe he's spoken to you about some of it.'

Nik Man stared down. He clearly wasn't going to say anything more.

'Never mind,' Maryam said, rising. 'Think about it. When you're ready to talk, you can get in touch with us.'

They thanked him for the coffee, and left, though Nik Man had hardly moved in his seat.

* * *

'Well, what do you think?' Rubiah asked as they began strolling back to their own kampong. She was anxious to begin the debriefing.

'Do you think Dris told him?'

Rubiah nodded. 'Absolutely. Otherwise he wouldn't have fallen apart the way he did. He knows all about it.'

'I agree. He does. But do you think he … reciprocates?'

Rubiah thought for a moment. 'I don't know. I don't think he wants to talk about it either way.'

'Of course not, he's afraid.'

'But taking him out of the equation altogether, do you think Dris might have killed Salim to protect Nik Man? Or, what I mean is, because Salim beat Nik Man and Dris was avenging him.'

'You know,' Maryam said thoughtfully, 'that could be the case whether or not Nik Man responded or not. His reaction might have nothing to do with how Dris would react.

'That's what I was thinking,' Rubiah agreed. 'It isn't so much an issue as to what Nik Man feels, but only what Dris does.'

Maryam nodded. 'Still, what do you think?'

Rubiah shook her head. 'He knows how Dris feels. I just don't know how he feels.'

Chapter XII

Rahman would have changed places with Maryam and Rubiah in a heartbeat. While they were considering Nik Man's state of mind, he was dragging from kampong to kampong, interviewing people who'd been at the contest in varying positions. Most of the people he spoke with regarded him with amazement when he asked them about it: 'I can hardly remember,' one kite flyer admitted. 'It's been a little while now and I'm vague on where everyone was.' Rahman was bitterly aware that he ought to have been doing this the moment after the murder was discovered, not after enough time had gone by that people could organize their alibis and conveniently not remember any of the details. He berated himself for not having thought of this earlier, and possibly allowing the guilty party to slip through their net just because they hadn't thought to ask until it was too late.

His overwhelming impression was of people's indifference to the murder. No one he spoke to seemed to be touched by Salim's demise: some were sympathetic, some overtly indifferent, but no one was really touched. The common impression was that he was a self-important loudmouth – both attributes being an anathema in Malay culture. Salim seemed to embody everything that people did not like. It was a shame that would be his only epitaph, Rahman thought.

One older man, who had been at the contest with his son, one of the most famous flyers in the area, chuckled when asked about the contest. 'A lot going on,' he mused. 'A murder. Well! I never expected to see that at a kite flying contest.' He sat on the steps of his porch, dressed in a sarong and undershirt, and invited Rahman and his junior to sit next to him and have a smoke. 'Kind of hot to be running around from house to house, eh? I don't envy you.' He took a deep, satisfying pull on his cigarette and looked out at the yard.

'I just can't understand how someone would kill over a contest.'

'Maybe it was for another reason,' Rahman offered.

'I don't know,' the man ruminated. 'Then why do it there? Anyway, and this is what I'm sure you want to know, I was watching my son fly, and then this Salim, his kite cut Nik Man's. I've known Nik Man from contests, and he's a good flyer, though I can't say I know him well. He was mad. I don't blame him. Salim was carrying on, whooping and shouting – you just don't do that. No one does that. I could see Nik Man wanted to … well, I don't know what he wanted to do but he was angry. I was watching because I was waiting to see someone land a punch.

'That didn't happen, at least while I saw them. And then, in a couple of minutes, the contest was over and Salim had won. Plenty of people were furious, I can tell you.' He shook his head. 'He was goading each one who hadn't won, people who were much better flyers than he was. And each one looked at him as if he'd love to see him dead, but they all walked away. Of course,' he added philosophically, 'someone did kill him, but he deserved it.

'I did see Nik Man talk to another man, after the contest was over, and it looked like an argument. I wasn't close enough to hear anything, but they were waving their arms like you do when you're having a fight.

'I wasn't paying that much attention when my son came back to me and we left. If I'd known someone was going to kill him, I would definitely have watched.' He laughed. Rahman noted he too did not seem that upset at Salim's death, and seemed to be saying it was justified. What was it about this man that made him so universally hated? It was the hooting and gloating, Rahman decided. No one could stand such provocation.

'I don't know if Nik Man had any more reason to kill him that anyone else there,' the man added.

Rahman looked surprised. 'Why Nik Man?'

The man rolled his eyes. 'Isn't that who you're thinking killed him? Isn't that what you're asking? He may have,' he said judiciously. 'And then again, he may not. If you took a poll at the contest on who wanted Salim dead, I can't think of anyone who would have said no. They just might not have wanted to do it themselves.'

* * *

Rahman walked thoughtfully back to the car with Zul, his junior, who had just joined the force straight from high school, which made him about 19 years old. Everything about police work delighted Zul, who constantly smoothed his tie and rearranged his cap. Everything relating to police work thrilled him: *laksana katak: sikit hujan, banyak bermain*: like a frog, showing much joy over a little rain. Zul's black curly hair falling into his eyes and his energetic walk led Rahman to remember his first years on the force and acknowledged he'd probably been as bouncy as Zul was now.

'What do you think?' Zul asked breathlessly. He asked everything breathlessly.

'It doesn't sound as if anyone liked him.'

'No one we've met had anything good to say about him,' Zul confirmed. 'He must have been something.'

Rahman agreed. 'I see that everyone had a reason to kill him, or at least some kind of motive, but someone actually took it to heart.'

'Do you think it was Nik Man?' bounced Zul. 'Could be.'

'Could be almost anyone,' Rahman said sadly. 'I wish I knew who.'

'Do you know who I think it was?'

'Who?'

'Omar, the bomoh.'

'Really?' Rahman was interested.

'He had a reason,' Zul recounted, 'because Salim told Nik Man about the jampi. And he's a bomoh.'

'And that means he'd kill someone.'

'No,' said Zul slowly, 'but it means he's used to life and death and this could have made him think someone needed to get rid of Salim.'

'A lot of people felt that way.'

'I know,' Zul agreed. 'But most of them wouldn't actually do it, you see. But a bomoh, they know about these things. They aren't scared of death like some people are.'

Rahman considered this while he turned on the car and turned onto the main road. 'You might be right,' he told him, and the praise made Zul beam and bounce at the same time. Rahman couldn't help but laugh.

'We should talk to Chief Osman about it.' Zul said nothing, but his smile got wider, if such a thing was possible, and he looked though he might levitate at any moment.

Chapter XIII

Rubiah and Maryam wandered through the narrow dirt paths of Kampong Banggol, weaving past other houses and yards, looking for anyone, preferably a woman, outside and available for a chat. Their first two attempts were met with glacial smiles and professed desolation that the press of chores was too much to be put aside, even for a moment, but on the third try, an older woman weaving a palm mat seemed delighted at a possible interruption, and invited them to sit down and have a smoke. They of course, promptly agreed.

'Investigating a murder, are you?' the woman seemed interested. 'Salim? The one killed at the kite flying contest?'

They nodded.

'I heard you were talking to Dris about that,' she continued, looking at them with bright eyes under her expertly wrapped head cloth. 'Good place to start.'

'Why, Kakak?' Maryam asked, leaning in closer.

'Well, you know how close he and Nik Man were. Working together on the kite. Dris never moved past what he'd been as a kid. A helper. How many grown men do you know who are helpers? It's a strange thing ...'

'What? Tell me,' Maryam urged her.

'He'd do anything to stay close to Nik Man.'

Do you think Nik Man noticed it?'

She cackled. 'Of course he did! He used it when he had to. Keeping Dris as his servant. Did he know? How could he not?'

'Know about what?' Rubiah said innocently.

'You know what I mean,' the woman said sternly. 'You're investigating this crime, so it's too late to play stupid.'

Rubiah did not expect such a straightforward answer, and it showed on her face.

Another cackle. 'You didn't expect anyone to say anything, did you? I'm too old to play games like that. Everyone knew, though we didn't talk about it much. I mean his family, and all. Why bring it up? But then with Nik Man ... well, it all changed a bit.'

'Nik Man was also, you know,' Maryam fumbled for a polite way to say it. 'I thought maybe Dris was interested but not Nik Man.'

The woman shrugged. 'I don't know how not interested he was. He had a good marriage, it seemed. But he certainly wasn't fighting Dris off.'

She smiled, but didn't cackle again, thankfully. 'Maybe you're looking at this the wrong way. If you want my opinion ...'

'We do,' Maryam assured her, though she was quite sure they would get it even if they didn't.

She took a deep drag on her cigarette and examined the mat she was weaving. 'I don't know this, mind you, but Salim, being who he was, he might have been threatening Dris, you know, to go to the police. Or maybe Nik Man heard he was threatening Dris ...'

'Blackmail?' Rubiah said.

'He was that kind of man,' she said.

Rubiah nodded. 'It would make sense.'

'Of course it would,' the woman answered with asperity. 'Salim threatens one of them, or both, and they decide to get rid of him. Do you see anyone mourning for Salim? And you won't. His wife isn't even that upset.' She started weaving her mat again.

* * *

Maryam returned home to sleep for more than twelve hours, almost a record for a wife and mother in Kelantan. She rose the next morning to preside over her stall with enthusiasm, happy to clear her mind of murder and concentrate instead on selling excellent quality Kampong Penambang *kain songket*, and batik her older brother Malek made himself. She sat contentedly on the platform of her stall, her small cardboard box which served as her cash register next to her, her hand rolled cigarettes and a box of matches in front of her, and the swirl and eddy of the *pasar besar,* the main market, of Kota Bharu surrounding her. She was home again.

In high spirits, she called to possible customers, beckoning them to see what she had for sale, of the highest quality, suitable for any bride. Which reminded her once more that Aliza wanted her wedding songket to be white with gold accents, a colour Maryam thought she'd gotten from looking at pictures of western wedding dresses. It would not necessarily have been Maryam's first choice but she'd long since learned, selling songket to brides and their mothers, that the bride's choice would prevail. And Aliza would look lovely in anything, and white would look fresh and cool. She had a piece she'd been saving, but the crush of the last week or so had pushed it out of her mind, and she knew it was time to bring this fabric to Aliza's attention so they could begin preparing the outfit.

Ashikin suddenly appeared in from of her, emerging from the crowd, smiling and looking beautiful, one child on her hip and the other holding her hand. 'I thought you'd be looking happy to be back,' she greeted her mother while handing over Zakaria, the baby. Nuraini, the reluctant older sister, immediately demanded to be picked up as well, to sit next to her grandmother and help run the stall.

'Aren't you working today?' Maryam asked.

'I'm working, just not right now,' she replied. 'When I get back to the store, Daud's mother will take them home.' Ashikin worked with her husband's family in their kain songket and batik store, and there was a playful, or not so playful, rivalry between the two sets of grandparents for their grandchildren's attention. Nuraini had become more demanding since her baby brother was born, in order to ensure she retained her status as queen of all she surveyed. She was a particular favourite of her grandfather Mamat, who saw in her Ashikin as a baby, and knew she'd grow up to look just like her mother.

'Maybe you could take at least Nuraini over to see Ayah,' Maryam suggested. 'He hasn't really gotten over the bird. He isn't himself and you know how he adores Aini. An afternoon with her would really cheer him up.' She dandled the baby on her lap, earning a scowl from Nuraini.

'She's really got to get over his,' Ashikin commented. 'You know, she can't spend the rest of her life jealous over her *adik-adik.* And she still doesn't like anyone paying attention to Zakaria.'

Maryam refused to be cowed by Nuraini's clear displeasure. 'I see. Jealous, are you?' She asked Nuraini with a smile, but the child refused to answer. 'And such a sweet little boy that you're jealous of,' she continued.

'Nuraini, listen to your *Nenek,*' her mother commanded. Nuraini turned her head away. 'If you don't want to talk, that's alright,' Ashikin continued, keeping her voice soft, 'then you can just get down from there and leave Nenek alone, if you aren't going to talk to her. It isn't nice, is it, Nenek?'

Maryam shook her head. 'No indeed, for such a big grown up girl like you to be jealous of a baby like Zakaria, I just don't understand it.'

'I want to see '*Tok,*' Nuraini said suddenly, having thought of someone who wouldn't give her lessons in deportment. 'Let's go and see him,' she turned to her mother.

'And take your adik?' Ashikin asked.

This was clearly not her first choice, but she bowed to the inevitable with what passed for good grace, and Ashikin grinned at her mother. 'I'm off to see Ayah,' she told her. 'I hope she cheers him up!'

Maryam watched them disappear into the market, and was soon distracted by a bride and her mother, eagerly looking through the songket, holding it up against the bride's face to see how it would bring out her eyes. Maryam dived into the discussion, pulling out possible pieces of cloth, congratulating the bride on her choice of light blue, which was very flattering. Bargaining commenced with each side settling down to enjoy it, in serious but good-natured fun. The bride stayed silent as she left the details to her mother; in the middle of the match, Maryam asked if they'd like some refreshment (bargaining could be hard work), and sent the bride upstairs to Rubiah's stall to have some coffee and cakes catered. Rubiah accompanied the girl back, and joined the discussion, which took far longer than it usually did, but in their relief to get back to daily life, both Maryam and Rubiah thoroughly enjoyed it.

At the end of the discussion, when the price had been agreed upon and the transaction finished, Maryam pulled out the white songket she was saving for Aliza. She was so proud of it, though she assured the bride in front of her the songket she'd bought was just perfect for her. 'You don't see white that much,' the mother commented, 'but this is beautiful. So cool, don't you think?'

'That's just what I thought,' Maryam stated proudly. 'Exactly what I thought.'

Chapter XIV

In the midst of tragedy and murder, life still went on, and Aliza was still going to be married. She liked the songket Maryam had chosen, much to her mother's pride and, though she didn't mention it, relief. The seamstress had been called in, the wedding outfit was now in production, and Ashikin was running the wedding planning with Rosnah, her sister-in-law, as her lieutenant.

At the beginning, they would call upon Aliza to make decisions, to pick out ornaments and discuss party favours.

'Adik!' Ashikin ordered her. 'Either you pay attention, or I'm just going to decide everything and when you come to your wedding, I don't want to hear any complaining.'

'I wouldn't dare,' Aliza assured her. 'Besides, you know what I like better than I do.'

'I know,' Ashikin agreed with no irony whatsoever. 'You like what I tell you to like.'

'You always have,' Aliza nodded. 'Why stop now?'

'You're right,' Ashikin said, realizing this was entirely for the best. Now she'd have a free hand without wasting any time conferring with the bride. Everyone would be happy.

Aliza and Ashikin's older brother Azmi had taken on Rahman,

and they bonded over their experiences as policemen and soldiers, which didn't seem so different when they compared notes. Rahman welcomed being part of Aliza's family, watching Maryam work up close. He had been somewhat in awe of her: taking on crime investigation and being so successful at it, and it cheered him to see her do what he thought of as 'normal' things, like cooking and cleaning and getting Yi off to school. He admired her ability to do so many things at the same time, and more to the point, her ability to delegate quickly and efficiently, keeping everything going at the same time. He could easily imagine Aliza running her household that way, with his daughters taking on tasks for their mother and his sons making more work for everyone. He sighed happily at the thought of his own family to come, himself as husband and father. He really couldn't wait.

Rahman sought to make Aliza proud of him, feeling that any heroism he displayed was now in the past, and some new heroics were probably in order. Had he mentioned this to Aliza, she would have been horrified: the thought of Rahman putting himself in danger was her greatest nightmare. Though she did think about their partnership after they were married: he as a policeman, she as the detective like her mother. It could work well, just look at Osman and Azrina. Osman enjoyed Azrina's insights and was proud of her abilities. Aliza could see he did, and hoped that Rahman would evince the same pride when she offered him her deductions. She was confident he would.

* * *

Mamat came back to the house with Nuraini, kidnapped from her parents for some quality time with Tok. She was delighted: her baby brother was at home and there was no one with whom she would need share the spotlight. Her grandparents, Aliza and Yi would pay attention only to her. In such a situation she could afford to be gracious, and on her best behaviour. She fairly danced around the house, watching TV with Yi, demanding to see pictures of the wedding dress with Aliza, sitting on Mamat's lap waiting for dinner to be served. It was precisely as she thought her life should be.

This dinner table was how Maryam thought her life should be: everyone healthy, grandchildren on Mamat's lap, Aliza looking forward to her wedding, and perhaps more grandchildren to come. Even though it was a peaceful scene, the case still worried her, as did anything she felt defied explanation. She began to get an inward glancing look on her face, and Aliza pulled her up short. 'Mak,' she said sternly, 'you're thinking about the case again. I can see it on your face.'

Maryam looked abashed. She didn't want this case to spoil everything else in her life. 'I'm sorry, I shouldn't be thinking about it now, you're right.'

'But what's worrying you?' Aliza stopped. 'Everything, right? You're worried about why it still seems unclear, and you think there's one answer to everything.'

Maryam looked at her; surprised she could sum it all up so neatly. 'Yes, to all of it,' she said. 'How did you know?'

Aliza grinned. 'I was thinking the same thing myself.'

'Let's not talk about this over dinner,' Mamat warned them.

'This one,' he nodded at Nuraini, 'will tell the whole kampong anything she hears, whether she understands it or not.'

'No, I won't,' she cried, with an unerring instinct for being discussed. 'I'm not a baby.'

'Of course you aren't,' Maryam said briskly. 'Would a baby be able to sit at the table like this? Of course not.' She served her some rice. She looked at Aliza telegraphing they would talk later. It was uncanny how Aliza came to so many of the same conclusions that she did.

After dinner, Ashikin stopped over to take Nuraini back, though she suggested Mamat might like to keep her for a while. The princess was not yet ready to leave, so Maryam sat outside in the cooling evening with her daughters, relaxed now, and ready to have thoughts just come into her mind rather than will them.

'So much all tangled up,' Maryam murmured, feeling far to lazy to really think hard. Luckily, both her daughters were prepared to think for her, so she was able to relax. Ashikin took the lead, as she was wont to do, because she had children to take care of and little time for wool gathering even in a good cause.

'You're working with Mak now?' she asked Aliza.

'Yes, I guess so,' Aliza replied, while at the same time her mother said 'Not really.' 'Aliza has a lot to worry about right now,' Maryam continued to explain, 'and she can't really spend the time to do this as well.'

'And anyway,' Ashikin added with her almost supernatural ability to predict what her parents were thinking, 'you don't want her to take the chance of getting hurt again. Especially not now, before the wedding. After the wedding it's Rahman's problem.'

She laughed softly, but Maryam frowned at her. 'No,' she began, but Ashikin cut her off.

'I'm only teasing, Mak. Don't be so worried. But of course, we'd all like this case wrapped up quickly so we'll have time before the wedding. I don't want the bride rushing in straight from an interrogation with her clothes askew.' Trust Ashikin to get to the heart of the matter, Maryam thought. Yes, it must be taken care of by the time of the wedding at least! Or sooner, which would be better.

'So, I will try to help, though I don't have that much time. What with the kids and all.' She waved an airy hand. 'And I have news: I wanted to tell you two alone first …'

'You're having another baby,' Aliza guessed.

'I can't believe you!' Ashikin was annoyed. 'Why don't you let me tell?'

'Oh, I'm so happy!' Maryam hugged her and laughed. 'Oh Ashikin, how wonderful.'

'I forgive you,' she told Aliza, who laughed at her.

'When?'

'In six months, I think. And guess who else, no wait! No guessing, I'll tell you. Rosnah! But when she tells you, you have to act surprised! Don't say you know!'

'Of course not,' Maryam assured her. Her spirits soared. How wonderful life was becoming!

Smiling all around, Ashikin brought them back to business, while Aliza went to get her a drink and a pillow for her back. 'Take advantage of it,' Maryam advised her. 'It won't be too long before she'll be having kids herself and you'll be bringing pillows.'

'And I'll be happy to do it. Then all we need to do is get Yi married.' They both considered this for a moment as Aliza returned. 'Did I hear you say you're going to get Yi married? It's hard to consider seriously yet. I mean, look at him.'

'I know,' Ashikin agreed, drinking her tea. 'But maybe in a few years he'll improve – you know, fill out and get smarter.'

'Maybe.' Aliza said dubiously.

'Everyone does,' Maryam answered, 'in the end.'

'He might not,' Aliza informed her mother. 'He might be one of the few who stays fifteen for his whole life. And then I'll have to take him when he grows up and he'll live with me and sleep in the kitchen.'

'Sounds perfect,' Maryam commented. 'I'll let him know. He'll be so pleased, don't you think?'

'That's enough about Yi,' Ashikin ordered. 'Someday he'll grow up, we just have to wait patiently.'

'Did you worry about Azmi this way?' Aliza asked.

'Azmi was different,' Maryam remembered. 'He seemed to grow up more quickly than Yi.'

'He was more handsome,' Aliza opined.

'He was the oldest,' Ashikin clarified. 'Yi's the baby. And you know, the youngest always takes more time to grow up. Everyone knows that.'

'Do they?' Aliza asked, and it was unclear to Ashikin whether the questions were about the youngest growing up more slowly or whether everyone knew that. Knowing Aliza, it could well be either one.

'OK,' Aliza said to Ashikin, taking over, 'this is where the case stands now.' In a few short sentences she summed up all the unravelled strands of the case. 'Could be Salim was killed because he won over Nik Man and made him furious. Or, Dris killed him because he beat Nik Man. Or Dris killed him because he was blackmailing him, or Nik Man because he was blackmailing Dris. And that's just the two of them.

'Omar because Salim told Nik Man he'd given him jampi, and Halimah because she hated him and now she had the land. It's amazing he's lived this long, with all the trouble he's caused.'

'Are there any suspects you particularly like?' Aliza asked her.

Ashikin thought for a moment, and rubbed her back. 'I like all of them,' she said finally. 'But I like Dris best because he had the most number of reasons, poor thing. Though I wouldn't blame him at all for killing Salim, if he did, especially if he was being blackmailed.' She stood up and called for Nuraini. 'You should check that out,' she ordered her sister. 'See if he was blackmailed.' And with smiles all around, she and Nuraini strolled home.

'How does she always know everything?' Aliza asked her mother, picking up the coffee cups. 'It isn't fair.'

Chapter XV

It might not have been fair, but Aliza followed her older sister's commands, and went with her mother to speak to Osman. Rahman sat in as well, full of pride seeing Aliza working with her mother, and she stole glances at him, smiling, which Osman and Maryam ignored.

'Blackmail?' Osman said. 'You know, I hadn't really thought about that, but it's a good angle. Do you think Dris would tell us if he was?'

'Maybe Dris wouldn't,' Aliza said suddenly, 'but maybe Halimah would. I don't think it would bother her to say something bad about Salim, if it were true,' she amended hastily.

Osman nodded. 'Should we talk to her?'

Maryam nodded. 'Sooner rather than later. How about today?'

Aliza was already on her feet. 'You and Rahman go,' Osman waved his hand munificently, but Maryam stood immediately. 'I want to go also and see what she says,' she said airily. Aliza grinned at her mother's chaperonage, raised her eyebrows at Rahman, and they left.

Halimah was still friendly when they arrived, though not quite as friendly as she had been before at her daughter's house. She greeted them politely and invited them up, and after the introductory serving and chitchat, she sat and waited for them to state their business.

'This is kind of delicate,' Maryam began, as Aliza looked modestly at her feet, and Rahman tried to look completely professional and impassive. 'You know, in investigating this, I began to wonder, difficult as Salim was, did he ever ... threaten Dris? About how he felt about Nik Man?' Maryam was relieved to have finished this, and sighed audibly.

'You mean blackmail?' Halimah asked.

'Yes.' She was so happy to get that word out of the way.

'I don't know,' she said, thinking. 'He certainly might have, he was like that. Dris never mentioned anything, nor did Latifah, though of course even if it happened they might not have said anything.' She looked at Maryam. 'Are you thinking Dris killed him for blackmail?'

Maryam shrugged. 'It's a thought.'

'Would you blame him if he did? He could ruin Dris' whole life. *Potong hidung, rosak muka:* cut off the nose and you destroy the face. You know,' she explained, 'people probably knew in the kampong, just knowing Dris and seeing him with Nik Man. People can draw their own conclusions. But it's different if it's announced, if everyone has to acknowledge it. It could become a religious thing – you know what I mean. We're all happy to ignore it, especially since, well,' she hesitated, 'he's married, he lives a quiet life. But if it's all out there, people will feel they have to disapprove. You know how it is.'

Maryam nodded. 'Of course.'

'So, I don't know if Salim tried to blackmail him. I'd detest him even more if he did. Poor Dris,' she commiserated. 'I hope it wasn't true. I can't imagine how Dris would feel, so ... trapped.'

Maryam nodded, again. 'It would be unbearable.'

Halimah said, 'If I were Dris, and he were blackmailing me, I don't know what I'd do. But I'm not saying Salim was doing it, because I don't know, and I don't want to make it seem like Dris killed him.' She shook her head hopelessly. 'What a mess.'

'I notice,' Maryam said drily, 'You didn't say that Salim was blackmailing Dris ...'

'To make him look guilty?' Halimah asked calmly.

'Yes, that.'

'Why?' She shrugged. 'If Dris did it, you'll find out about it. I don't doubt you for a moment. And if he didn't, why would I want to accuse him with no reason?'

'Some might say to take suspicion off yourself.'

'They might, but they'd be wrong. If I said he did, you'd start wondering soon enough if it was true or not, and when you found out I lied ...' She stopped and took a sip of her coffee. 'When you found that out, I'd be in real trouble. Why would I get into that? I wouldn't,' she answered her own question. 'I'll keep to the truth, thank you.' She seemed to have completely lost interest in the conversation.

'Why don't you ask Dris? He might say no and then you

wouldn't know what to think, would you? Well, it certainly is a problem,' she said, revealing no sympathy in her tone. 'I wouldn't want your job, but then, you do seem to enjoy it, so maybe it isn't as bad as all that.' She turned to Aliza. 'Are you following your mother into detecting?'

Aliza smiled and looked pleased. 'I think so.'

'Well, just be careful,' Halimah admonished her. 'These situations can be dangerous.' She rose to bid them farewell. 'You don't talk too much, do you?' she asked Rahman with visible amusement. 'Very polite.'

'Well, I …' He began to explain and then realized he wasn't sure how to explain it, or what indeed he was clarifying, so he stopped speaking. Maryam looked at him approvingly, and Aliza lovingly, and that ended the interrogation.

'Wait a minute, please,' Maryam said suddenly. 'Do you think Salim might have tried to threaten Nik Man?'

'But I don't think he's …'

'Perhaps not. But if Salim started talking about it, it might not only hurt Dris, but Nik Man and his family as well. Couldn't it?'

'Of course. You know it would be a huge scandal and everyone involved would be affected. I don't see Salim having the nerve to approach Nik Man like that – Nik Man would never stand for it. Dris was the weaker of the two, and the more … guilty, I suppose.'

Maryam thanked, her, and turned again, just as she was leaving, as though she'd just remembered something to ask. 'Kakak, do you know anything about birds?'

Halimah looked mystified. 'Birds?'

'Songbirds. Merbok.'

'No.' She didn't look the least bit shaken, just confused. 'Should I?'

'Just asking.' Maryam stayed deep in thought all the way back to the car.

Chapter XVI

'I never considered it before,' she told Rahman and Aliza as they drove back to Kampong Penambang. 'He could easily have threatened Dris, but by doing that he was indirectly threatening Nik Man and his family. You know how stories start, it would be all over Kelantan in no time at all if people started talking about it.'

Aliza looked thoughtful. 'It's another motive for Nik Man.'

'And his family,' Maryam added. 'His wife and her older sister who we met at her house. She was furious, and she hated Dris. She's the first who ever mentioned Dris was in love. Could she have gone over to the contest and killed Salim?'

'Why not kill Dris?'

'If Salim was threatening Dris, it was Salim who'd spread the story, not Dris. Maybe she was angry at Dris for putting them all in such a vulnerable situation.'

'It could be,' Rahman agreed, 'but who's going to admit it now?'

'That's just it,' she murmured, wishing Rubiah were here. 'I don't see the family deciding they need to talk about it. Can you ask whether anyone saw Bahiyah at the contest? Bring her picture around?'

Rahman agreed, that he and Zul could probably go back, house to house with a picture, and see if anyone identified her. Maryam decided that she and Rubiah could go to see Bahiyah and Sharifah directly, and see if any new information was forthcoming.

They could see they had definitively worn out their welcome at Nik Man and Sharifah's home. Sharifah was outside in the back, doing laundry at the well, and was in no mood to accompany Maryam and Rubiah on another meandering conversation which seemed to be going nowhere, and as far as she could see, no closer to solving the crime. She looked up at them but did not stop washing, leaving them to talk to her while she got through her chores. And, even more telling, she did not interrupt her work to offer any refreshment. She'd been polite long enough – longer than necessary really, what with discussions about Salim and then listing everyone Nik Man remembered at the contest. She had work to do and a house to run, and was too busy to indulge in criminal speculation.

She sat on her haunches with a large plastic tub in front of her, filled with soapy water, and she scrubbed her clothes with a vengeance. 'Good morning, Mak Cik,' she said shortly, without pausing in her work. 'What brings you here?'

'Just a question or two,' Rubiah said as nicely as she could, and was rewarded with a very sharp look but no comment. The sound of the brush against the wet laundry continued unabated.

'Did your sister ever go to kite flying contests with you?'

'No.'

'Did she ever go at all?'

'No.'

'Does she like kite flying? Is she interested in it?'

'No.'

Sharifah took a bucket full of clean water and dumped it over the newly washed clothes, and then went back to work again. She did not look up at them.

'Do you think it possible she might have gone?' Maryam tried.

'No.'

'Ever?'

'Why would she?'

'Just to see it.'

'What are you really asking me. Did my kakak go to the contest and kill Salim? No. I wasn't there. She wasn't there. You already know who was there. What else do you want?' She tried to keep herself from being angry. 'We've tried to answer all your questions and help you. You can't keep coming here all the time and asking more.' She was silent and stopped scrubbing for a moment. 'I mean, I suppose you can, since you're working for the police but really, is it necessary? I don't know what else to tell you.' She squared her shoulders and resumed cleaning. 'Is that all you wanted?'

'What do you know about merbok?' Maryam asked as she prepared to leave.

Sharifah squinted at them. 'Merbok?'

'Yes. Songbirds. My husband raises them.'

Sharifah said nothing and turned away from them. Maryam and Rubiah knew they'd get nothing out of her now, but could easily do some damage by avoiding a tactical retreat. They smiled and backed off, walking down the lane hoping to run into Bahiyah.

They planted themselves at the small, rickety coffee bar at the end of the path along the main road, where they would be very visible and possibly the topic of conversation. They ordered iced coffee and some curry puffs, though Rubiah really disliked eating any Malay pastries other than her own. The quality just wasn't there, she thought, and why eat sub-optimal pastries? However, she was on the job, and this was just one of the sacrifices one made. She stirred her coffee with resignation.

Maryam kept up a steady stream of chatter with the owner of the stall, who was only too happy to gossip, especially at this time of day, which was usually so quiet. She finally moved the conversation around to Nik Man, Sharifah and her family, and was rewarded with some of the man's reminiscences.

'Well, Bahiyah, now she always did run the family. Sharifah is one of the younger ones – is she the youngest? I can't remember. But Bahiyah always protected her, even after she was married. Bahiyah always wanted to make sure Sharifah was all right, and Bahiyah has children of her own, you know! But I guess you get used to taking care of your younger brothers and sisters and you never get over it, right?'

Maryam agreed it was right.

'I mean now, Sharifah has children and a husband and doesn't really need looking after, not in the same way. But Bahiyah's very protective. And this murder – you know about the murder at the kite flying contests. The guy who was murdered, he lived here! Kampong Banggol is a real kite-flying village, it's our specialty, you might say. Every place has a specialty and ours is kites. Most of the men fly, and some are real champions. Like Nik Man. He's a winner, he flies so well. People like to go and see him, and the other guys who fly. You know, just to cheer on your own kampong. It's a great hobby, though I think a lot of guys make a pretty good living at it, too.

'Not this Salim, he was new to the sport. He was a difficult man. I don't want to speak badly of him, but he could be difficult. Most of the other men aren't, they're nice and polite like you'd expect …'

Behind him, Bahiyah loomed, like a shark appearing at a reef.

'Che Awang! Gossiping again, telling everyone all about our kampong and people who live in it.' It was clearly not the first time Bahiyah had been irritated by the coffeeshop owner's garrulous conversation. 'They're working for the police and you're just talking away!'

'It was just talk, kakak,' Maryam tried to soothe her, but she was having none of it.

'Just talk that didn't need to be spread.' The owner was trying his best to recede into the wall, away from Bahiyah's line of fire. He began drying already dry coffee cups.

'People are allowed to talk,' Rubiah said as mildly as she could. 'It was harmless.'

'Why are you here?'

'How did you know we were here?' Rubiah countered.

'I just saw Sharifah and she told me you'd been by again, to bother her. I thought you were solving crimes! Then solve them please, and stop interrupting everyone's day.' She stood there, implacable, intimidating the coffee stall owner, but not cowing Maryam and Rubiah.

'Why are you so angry?' Maryam asked. 'We are allowed to speak with Sharifah in the course of the investigation. You know there are only a few suspects.'

Bahiyah snorted. 'I'm angry because you're bothering us. And I want …'

Maryam did not find out what Bahiyah wanted because Rubiah interrupted in a calm yet forceful way. 'We aren't bothering you,' Rubiah enunciated very clearly. 'We are working to solve a crime: the murder of someone from this very kampong, and you of all people should be anxious for us to do it as quickly as we can. The police are working, we're working, and I would expect you'd try to help as much as you could to find the killer. How can you complain about being bothered in a time like this?'

Another woman might have been abashed after a lecture like that, or might at least have given grudging acceptance, but Bahiyah was not the kind to yield. Maryam privately wondered what her marriage was like if she was this unmovable over everything. However, that was really out of her purview. Right now, she just hoped to find out Bahiyah was at the contest, though it seemed unlikely. Unfortunately.

Bahiyah stood her ground, arms akimbo, until Rubiah suggested they adjourn to a more private place for a talk. Bahiyah agreed, and after favouring the stall owner with a sulphurous look, they walked in silence to Bahiyah's house.

'Why are you so angry with us?' Rubiah asked, determined to get to the heart of the matter, rather than politely trying to ignore it.

'I don't see why you're hanging around here,' she scolded, 'we didn't kill Salim. Why don't you find who did?'

'Like Dris?'

'Exactly. And not Nik Man or Sharifah.'

'Or you,' Rubiah answered boldly.

'Me?' She was flabbergasted. 'How could it be me?'

'How?' Rubiah asked, now thoroughly annoyed. 'I'll tell you how.' Maryam tried to place a calming and restraining hand on her arm, but Rubiah shook it off. 'You've heard that Salim warned Dris he'd tell everyone how he felt about Nik Mat, and you were panicked,' Bahiyah snorted at the thought of her panicking, and Rubiah ignored it. 'Yes, I said panicked. So you went to the contest to shut him up. Did you argue with him there, in the bushes where no one saw you? Or did you just grab the string and kill him? I'm not sure yet. You did it to protect your sister, I know. But you wanted to know how could it be you? That's how.' Rubiah was stern, unbending, and yet pleased with herself for replying to this woman on her own terms.

It was Maryam's turn to be astounded, now. She'd been thinking it, but she hadn't organized it that well yet, and listening to Rubiah outline her theory, it made a great deal of sense. She watched Bahiyah for signs of cracking: nervousness, fear, even fury, but saw none of them. Something resembling hatred, yes, that was there, but it wasn't directed at Salim.

'You,' she said to Rubiah, with contempt. 'You with your theories. And the police. I don't know what's become of Kelantan.'

'What is it you think has become of it? We're still interested in justice, here.' Rubiah simply refused to retreat. It was something to see.

'You don't know what you're talking about.'

'Don't I? Then explain it to me. I came here hoping to hear it.' Rubiah watched her defiantly.

Bahiyah took a deep breath, more to keep her from smacking Rubiah than to actually calm herself, Maryam calculated, but still, better than a fistfight between two mak ciks. It would only be a scandal and one of them could easily be hurt, even by accident.

'Why would I kill Salim?' Bahiyah demanded rhetorically. 'He wasn't a threat to Nik Man or Sharifah, or me,' she added witheringly, with a disgusted look at Rubiah. 'That Dris, a useless man, always trailing after Nik Man like a *kerbau cucok hidung*: like a buffalo with a ring through its nose. I'm not sure Nik Man even noticed that.' Maryam was sure that Nik Man had indeed noticed it, but let Bahiyah go on with her version of events, which promised to be quite revealing of Bahiyah's thought process if nothing else.

'I hated him hanging around. I could see how he looked at Sharifah.'

'Sharifah?'

'Yes, of course, what do you think?'

'I thought Nik Man.'

Bahiyah gave a hoarse bark of a laugh and a mirthless smile. 'Nik Man? Don't be crazy.'

'Why? That's what I've heard.'

'I don't know where you heard it,' she shook her head. 'Do you think Nik Man would be mixed up with something like that?

With a wife like Sharifah? I don't know what goes on in Kampong Penambang …'

'I am saying,' Rubiah said loudly, gritting her teeth, 'that I have heard that Dris was interested in Nik Man.' She suddenly realized what she was saying and looked around them. They were standing at the bottom of the stairs to Bahiyah's porch, and it occurred to Rubiah they might actually be having this conversation with all her neighbours. She cleared her throat and pitched her voice to be far quieter. 'Have you heard that?'

Bahiyah's face turned a dark red. 'Maybe,' she said stiffly. 'But it's crazy rumours.'

'It's crazy rumours about him and Sharifah too, isn't it?' Rubiah pursued. 'I mean, he may have looked at her, but she …'

'Would never have looked back,' Bahiyah said firmly. 'Don't even think it.'

'I'm not thinking it,' Rubiah said impatiently, 'I'm saying the rumour is that Dris was in love with Nik Man,'

'Alamak!' Bahiyah cried out.

'And not Sharifah,' Rubiah finished. 'And if so …'

'It would be horrible. A scandal. A sin.'

'Yes, well, that's not what I'm talking about. I'm asking whether you'd heard that rumour, and I'd say you had.'

Bahiyah turned to her, her eyes slits and her mouth tight. 'I never heard it,' she spit. 'And don't go around saying it, either. You could be ruining someone's life for no reason at all.'

'I'm not spreading it,' Rubiah answered with heat, and Maryam wondered whether she would be forced to physically separate them. And if she had to, could she? 'I'm asking you!

Again! For the last time! Did you hear something like that, and do you think Salim would have blackmailed Dris about it?'

Bahiyah was silent, as though someone had turned off the switch, and Maryam could almost hear her thinking. This theory led away from Nik Man and his family and toward Dris, whom Bahiyah did not like. Surely it was a more desired state of affairs for her to have Dris under suspicion than Nik Man. And yet, if this were true (and heaven knew Salim was more than capable of blackmail) might it not lead back to Nik Man somehow? And would Nik Man's reputation be tarnished by all this talk of a love affair (Alamak!) with another man.

Bahiyah turned this over in her mind, and Maryam was convinced that her calculations in no way turned on truth or falsehood, but rather what would be beneficial to her sister and her family. As a witness, Bahiyah would be most untrustworthy, since this would be her primary concern every time, and truth be damned. But as a killer, she'd be perfect.

Chapter XVII

'You were wonderful! Aliza, you should have seen your Mak Cik Rubiah. She was so brave, like a warrior! I just stood there with my mouth open and she would not back down!' She beamed at Rubiah, and told the story to anyone who would listen. Mamat sat at the table chuckling to hear it, and Abdullah, Rubiah's husband, was very proud, but probably the least surprised person in the room.

'You must have been wonderful,' Aliza said with enthusiasm. 'I'm so sorry I missed it.'

'It wasn't much …'

'Not much?' Maryam was indignant. 'It was amazing, that's what it was. *Duduk seperti kucing, melompat seperti harimau:* she sits like a cat and springs like a tiger! This woman had never had anyone tell her off before, not like that. Not with such intelligence and spirit. She didn't know what to say!'

Rubiah looked modestly down and helped herself to some more rice. 'Someone had to stand up to her. Such a bully! Really, she couldn't believe we weren't afraid of her.'

'Did she confess?' Aliza asked.

'No, not exactly,' Maryam admitted. 'But I think she's a

suspect now. I think she knows it too, she could see how she was admitting one thing after another. If I could only find someone who saw her at the contest, I'd say she did it. She has real nerve, too, and she won't crack out of guilt.'

'Guilt?' Rubiah snorted. 'She's never heard of it.'

'Have you heard anything from Rahman?' Rubiah asked Aliza. 'Wasn't he going to see whether he could find anyone who might have seen her there?'

'He's asking, but I haven't heard he's found anyone yet. It could still be her even if we can't find anyone who saw her.'

'Yes, it could be,' agreed Maryam, 'but it will be hard to prove and we really don't have anything on her if no one can place her there. And she isn't going to tell us, I'm quite sure of that.' Rubiah nodded.

'I'll mention it to him again,' Aliza said.

'No, don't,' her mother told her. 'He's already working on it, and you don't need to remind him. You're getting married in a few weeks, don't nag him now.'

'No,' her father advised her. 'Wait until after you're married.'

Yi began laughing and Aliza silenced him with a look. 'What do you think is so funny?'

'You and Rahman. Poor Rahman,' and he dashed from the table to avoid the slap coming his way. 'Alright now,' Mamat ordered. 'Yi, back to the table. Aliza, don't hit him. We didn't mean to tease you.' He made a face at Maryam and peace was re-established.

'Do you really think it's her?' Aliza took up the topic once more.

'Could be,' Rubiah said mildly. 'She'd certainly do it if she thought it would save her sister.'

'Do you think she'd kill Dris too?'

Rubiah considered it. 'Dris himself isn't so much of a threat,' she said finally. 'On his own. The threat would be if someone made it public, and that would be Salim, you see.'

'Would she kill a bird?'

They were all silent. Maryam stole a glance at Mamat, who looked down at his plate.

'She would,' Maryam said softly. 'Actually, any of them would if they were the killer and they wanted us to stop.'

'You're right,' Rubiah agreed.

Aliza regretted bringing up the merbok, which so upset her father. She cleared her throat to bring the conversation back to the less upsetting topic of the murder of Salim, aware of the strangeness of it, but her father, and probably all of them, felt more for the bird than they had for him. 'So there are three people who might have wanted to kill him for blackmail.'

'Possible blackmail.'

'Right. Nik Man, Dris and Bahiyah. Anyone else? Sharifah? Halimah?'

'I suppose logically …' Rubiah began.

'But is it likely?'

'We have no proof they were there.'

'But if they were …'

'Blackmail is a powerful motive. I read it somewhere.' Rubiah announced. 'Anyone who's pushed hard enough, or is frightened enough could kill.'

'All of them might have felt in danger from Salim, if indeed, he thought of it.'

'He sounds like he'd think of it faster than we did,' Aliza added. 'He sounds so mean.'

'That's what is sounds like,' her mother agreed, thinking.

'Should we concentrate on one motive at a time?' Aliza asked. 'You know, like blackmail first, losing the contest second, getting a divorce, third, losing your jampi business fourth.' That way we look at the motives which could apply to the most people first, and then, if we don't find the killer, each of the others only has one person involved.' Aliza looked expectantly around the table.

'Yes,' Rubiah said slowly, 'though the blackmail is going to be hardest. After all, who will admit to it? No one. We're going to have to trip someone up to find out if it happened, and if they're determined, and strong, we'll never find out.'

'Dris isn't that strong,' Maryam noted. 'He's the weakest one.'

*　*　*

Osman called Dris in to the police station, calculating it was far more intimidating than sitting in your own living room. And so it appeared: Dris looked troubled and nervous, and could hardly swallow his coffee. Osman felt sorry for him, until he remembered once more why he was there, and that stiffened his spine for his questioning.

'So, it's come to our attention,' Osman cleared his throat, 'that you may have been blackmailed by Che Salim, and that he was, in fact, threatening you.'

'With what?' Dris asked nervously.

Osman nearly rolled his eyes, but caught himself. 'Che Dris, what do you think? Didn't you tell us at your house?' He waited a moment, but Dris didn't acknowledge anything. 'Nik Man,' he said finally. 'Remember?'

'I remember,' he said softly. 'Yes.'

'And did Che Salim ...?'

'Did he what?'

'Blackmail you.'

Dris appeared to be having trouble following the conversation. 'About Nik Man?'

Osman didn't think he could answer without raising his voice, so he sat silent.

'That's what you're asking, isn't it?'

'Yes. I am asking you if Che Salim was blackmailing you because he knew you loved Nik Man. Is that clear enough?'

Dris gulped and nodded. 'Yes, I understand.'

'Was he?'

'Kind of.'

'What does that mean?'

Rahman, taking notes in the corner, looked up at Dris. How difficult was this to follow anyway? He wondered whether Dris was having a stroke, getting ready to die, and he steadied himself in case he needed to leap up and catch him.

'He said he might tell Latifah, my wife.' Osman nodded. 'I didn't know she already knew, you see. So I didn't want her to know. If I had known,' he looked at Osman confidentially, 'well, naturally I wouldn't have worried about it all. Not for a moment.

But I thought it would hurt her.' He spoke very quietly, almost to himself.

'And ...?' Osman prompted him gently.

'I asked him not to,' he answered. 'I told him Latifah might take it badly.' Osman could hardly believe what he was hearing. Take it badly? At the very least she'd take it badly.

'A good strategy,' Rahman congratulated him. 'You'd want to make sure he knew that.'

Dris turned to him gratefully. 'Thank you. I thought that as well – I mean, maybe he hadn't thought this through. If I pointed it out to him he might see it wasn't a very good idea.' Rahman nodded, and Osman began to feel he might have entered an alternate universe.

'Did you tell Nik Man about it?' Rahman encouraged him. 'He might have been able to talk to him.' Or kill him, either one.

'Well, that's the thing, you see. I think – though I can't be sure – that Salim already told Nik Man. And Sharifah.'

'Really?' Rahman was on the edge of his seat, while still remembering to take notes. 'How do you know that?'

'Bahiyah told me.'

Chapter XVIII

Osman and Rahman, Maryam, Rubiah, Aliza and Azrina converged upon the police station, where Nik Man, Sharifah and Bahiyah were present, though not to be questioned together. Zul, now in charge of snacks and coffee, as Rahman had previously been, was serving quietly, keeping as far away from Bahiyah as possible, much as one would have kept away from a growling tiger. It was clear she terrified him, and Rahman made a mental note to strengthen his nerve in the face of scary suspects. Bahiyah was well aware of her effect on him, and it encouraged her to dial it up rather than down.

Sharifah and Nik Man were quiet, speaking to no one, not even each other, but Bahiyah continued a constant stream of grumbling as she sat at the table. Osman waved Nik Man into his private office, and sat him in the middle of the group.

'Che Dris tells me that Salim told you both, or all three of you, please clarify that for me, that Dris was in love with you.'

Nik Man blushed to the tips of his ears, but said nothing. 'Did he?' Osman prodded him.

Nik Man squirmed in his seat and obviously wished to be anywhere but where he was, and finally, after what seemed like an eternity, he sighed, 'Yes.'

'When?'

'Maybe a day or two before the contest.'

'You didn't think this worth mentioning?'

Nik Man said nothing, as there was nothing to say.

'Tell me about it,' Osman said impatiently, listening to the low buzz of voices from the other rooms in the station.

Nik Man looked embarrassed. 'He came over to the house and sat down. We had to give him coffee, though I wanted to throw him out. You can't though, can you? You still have to be polite, and we were. And then he said, 'I guess you both know about Dris, right?' We asked him what and he smiled this wicked, awful smile at Sharifah and said, 'You know he's in love with your husband.' I don't think Sharifah did know; I'm not sure how much she took notice of Dris anyway. She was shocked. She looked at me and I told her, 'Wait a minute. Don't look at me. I don't love him, you know. Absolutely not. This is just something he's kept since he was a kid. Not love really, more like boyish hero worship.'

'"No, it's not that," Salim said. I could have killed him.' Nik Man did not seem to notice what he'd said. 'Sharifah,' I told her, 'whatever Dris thinks has nothing to do with me.' I stood up and told Salim to go. He kept drinking his coffee. Can you believe it? I told him: "Get out before I throw you out." He finally left. Sharifah ran out of the house to go talk to Bahiyah.' He sighed. 'You know, it wasn't as though I were the one in love with Dris. Believe me, Sharifah had nothing to be afraid of.'

'Did Bahiyah come over later?'

'Of course, what do you think? It was a mess, and I didn't even do anything!' The unfairness of it all seemed to sting. 'Bahiyah told me she'd always suspected Dris was in love with Sharifah, and didn't I think that too? It never occurred to me, really. But she kept carrying on, which is what she does, about how Dris was ruining our family and putting Sharifah and the kids in danger. "What danger?" I asked her. "Do you know Dris? Sharifah could knock him over with one good shove."

'"People will find out," she said. "You'll be the topic of gossip, and once they start talking about Dris loving you, soon enough it will turn around that you love him too. Is that what you want?" Of course it isn't what I want. Who would want something like that? But it isn't blackmail,' he assured them. 'Because he already told Sharifah, so there was nothing more to be done. I guess he was going to tell Latifah, too, and Bahiyah knew. It wouldn't be too long till everyone knew, I suppose,' he said morosely.

'And now?'

Nik Man shrugged. 'Now the scandal will be his murder. Anything he told anyone won't really matter. Now it's just gossip that some guy said. I'll deny it, Dris will deny it and Sharifah and Bahiyah will also ignore it.'

'Lucky for you he's dead.'

Nik Man looked straight at him. 'It's lucky for a lot of people.'

'Did you kill him?' Osman asked casually.

'No. But I'm glad he's dead.'

* * *

Dris was another kind of suspect altogether. Though Osman feared he'd lost his mind the last time he spoke to him, now he seemed just as rabbitty but more in control.

'So,' Osman began quietly, afraid of spooking him, thereby rendering him mute, 'So, apparently Salim was in the process of telling people.'

Dris nodded. There was no vagueness or inability to understand what Osman was saying to him. 'I know, I mean, I knew when Bahiyah told me, of course. That was Salim for you,' he said philosophically. 'He tells your secret before even asking you to do anything. It isn't really blackmail, is it, if he's already let it out?'

'I guess not.'

'Not that I have anything, so I don't know what he'd blackmail me for, but whatever it was, he didn't even ask for it. It was just doing ... harm, I guess. That's what he wanted to do. Not get money. I don't have any anyway, so if that's what he wanted he'd have to go after someone else. He just wanted to hurt me, hurt Nik Man, Sharifah, anyone he could.'

'You didn't say Latifah.'

'I just forgot.'

'Forgot your own wife? Don't you think she'd be hurt by it?'

'She knows already. It won't be a surprise to her.' He sounded beaten, finished.

'Couldn't she still be hurt when it became a topic of conversation?'

'Maybe. OK, so add her to the list.'

'I just wonder,' Osman mused, 'whether she felt this more

deeply than you seem to think.'

'What?' Dris no longer seemed to be paying close attention.

'She might have been far more reluctant for this to be kampong gossip than you seem to think.'

Dris said nothing.

'After all, if Sharifah would have been embarrassed, think how much worse it would be for Latifah.'

Dris looked as though his days of thinking about anything were over. He mumbled something that might have been 'yes'.

'Did you tell her Salim had told Nik Man?'

He shook his head. 'Sharifah did.'

Osman stared at him, and felt awash in pity for Latifah. How humiliating for her: he could imagine Sharifah berating her, and none of this was her fault. He was angry at Dris, not for what he did or didn't do regarding the murder, but because he cared not at all for his wife, who was struggling to make things work, and whose concern was wasted on her husband.

'Have you ever kept merbok?' Osman asked him.

Dris looked at him with dead eyes. 'Once. Not now.' He seemed to have no curiosity as to why Osman would ask that. It seemed cruel to keep asking him questions.

'Thanks. I'll talk to you again later.' Dris shuffled out to the main room and lit a cigarette, his eyes empty.

* * *

Latifah would not relish being the object of anyone's pity, he could see that: she was far more spirited than her husband, and in his own opinion, far too good for him. However, that was a reflection for another time.

'I understand, Cik Latifah, that Salim had already told Nik Man and Sharifah.'

'I heard. Sharifah came over to me right after she'd gone crying to Bahiyah. I felt bad, no one wants to be involved in something like that, but really, what did she want me to do about it? Did she think I wanted the world to know?

'Police Chief Osman,' she began formally, 'I don't know how people react in Perak,' why, thought Osman, did people here seem to thing Perak was another world? 'But here, people can be very tolerant of many things as long as they aren't forced to acknowledge it.' Osman nodded: Perak wasn't so different. 'People might have suspected about Dris, they might have known. But it wasn't "public", if you know what I mean, and Dris and I lived a very discreet life, you could say. We kept ourselves to ourselves.' She thought for a moment. 'What I mean is, Dris didn't ... he wasn't ... you know. So, everyone could ignore it and it all went well.

'Salim told Sharifah and if Bahiyah knew everyone would know and then no one could overlook it anymore. And if they had to see it, they'd have to disapprove. Things would change then. People would talk openly. What about my children? What about me? We might have to move somewhere else and how would we do that? Maybe it would be best for me to get a divorce. I think that would be better than trying to keep going with Dris. I don't know. That's not blackmail, though,' she said, echoing her husband. 'That's just vicious.'

'I have a motive for killing that man, but if I did it would be before he told people. It's already out, so what's the point?'

'Yes, but people are talking about his murder now, not about Dris.'

'True. Lucky for me. I'm glad he's dead.' That seemed to be the common emotion with everyone he spoke to.

'Did you kill him?'

She laughed. 'I wish I did.'

* * *

Omar walked in with more confidence than Dris or Latifah, and more buoyant, as well.

'Have you made it up with Nik Man?' Osman asked.

His face clouded. 'Not yet. He's still angry at me.'

'Do you think he'll get over it?'

'I don't know. I hope so. I mean, we've worked together for so long ...'

'And Salim won't have any business for you.'

Omar gave him a sour look. 'No he won't, but that's not the point.'

'What is the point?' Osman leaned forward. 'Tell me.'

'I just want to get back to working with Nik Man, that's all. Salim is of no consequence.'

'Well, now he isn't.'

'It was a mistake,' Omar was becoming annoyed. 'A mistake. I admit it. I should never have done anything with Salim and I'm very sorry for it, that's for sure. I hope Nik Man can forgive me, because I will never do anything like that again.'

Osman nodded.

'I'm sure not, but Salim kind of ruined your business, didn't he? If only he'd kept quiet.'

'Yes,' Omar agreed with spirit. 'I only wish he'd kept his mouth shut. But what can you do now?'

'Now? Nothing. But you could have done something when you first saw him do it.'

Omar thought for a minute. 'Kill him, you mean?'

Osman nodded.

Omar shrugged. 'Even then, it was already too late. I should have killed him before he started talking, if I had known that was what he was going to do. But it's too late for that, too, right?'

'Unless you did it,' Osman mused.

'Unless I did it,' he echoed, seemingly unconcerned. 'There are a few people right here who wish they'd killed him earlier. I don't know if there's anyone here who wishes he weren't dead.'

'That's not much of an eulogy.'

'No it isn't, but he wasn't much of a man, either.'

'I didn't know you'd hated him.'

'I didn't. But now that I know more, I do, a little. Well, if you think I did it, I don't know what to do. I didn't. But you'll have to convince yourself.'

'You sound like you're almost confessing.'

'I'm not. But I'm not being coy, either.'

'Would you prefer the investigation stopped?'

'Of course I would! Do you think I enjoy being brought in here and asked all these question?' he said scornfully. 'I'd be very happy if it stopped.'

'Don't you want to find out who killed him?'

'No, not really,' Omar said. 'I like all these people, and I wouldn't want any harm to come to them. And I don't care about Salim. So no.'

'You're honest.'

Omar shrugged. 'Anything else?'

'Yes, just one small thing. What do you know about merbok? You know, singing doves.'

Omar's reaction was surprising. A column of red came up his neck and into his face as he fought to keep it expressionless. Osman could have sworn he saw his eyes bulge as he gulped. 'Why?' he asked hoarsely, now looking frightened. 'Why would I know anything about them?'

'I'm just asking. One is involved in this case.'

'A bird?' he croaked.

Osman nodded. 'You know something about this, don't you?'

Omar rose. 'No. Can I leave now?'

'No, not yet. Sit down, and tell me the truth.'

'I didn't do anything to any birds.'

'But you do know someone who did, don't you?' Osman leaned in farther.

'No.' Omar had gotten control of himself now, and was stone faced and still.

'I'm going to assume it was you unless I find out otherwise,' Osman told him sternly. 'Which means, let me make clear to you, that you might be my favourite suspect for killing more than a bird. Think about it.'

He took Omar by his arm and led him out of the room. 'Put him in the back for now,' he told Rahman. Omar looked shocked, and sent a pleading look to Nik Man and Sharifah as Rahman took him to a cell. Without speaking, he closed the door and left, shooting back an accusatory look: after all, this was his father in law's bird.

He walked back into the room where Maryam was lecturing the assembled suspects. '… to hang a small defenceless bird, left there for her owner to find, this is an evil mind, one I would never have thought to see here in Kelantan.' She glared at the group before her. 'Someone wants this investigation stopped, and an innocent life means nothing to them. I can see, in a way,' she amended, 'how you would all feel about Salim, who didn't seem like a good person. But what could you possibly have against a singing bird? Tell me that!'

They all seemed to cringe in their seats, looking at no one, not even each other. But no one admitted to anything either.

Chapter XIX

Maryam did not like to think either Nik Man or Sharifah killed Salim, even less did she like to think they'd killed Mamat's bird. They had young children after all, and she hated the thought of those children losing their parents, or at least one of them. Of course, Dris had children too, but they were a bit older, and for reasons she could not accurately identify they didn't worry her as much.

The two widows, as she thought of them, would be excellent killers, without doubt. But she wasn't sure this crime was their kind of work. She envisioned them planning it carefully, doing it in a way that people might have thought it was a heart attack. They seemed supremely in control of themselves, and almost frighteningly practical. The hanging seemed a more impulsive act, done with materials at hand, perhaps not even planned. Though it was true anyone could be driven to any kind of crime, even a crime out of character.

But for off the cuff murder, done with little thought and less control, she liked Omar. Dris seemed too limp for murder, but Omar had some backbone, and Salim's last act on earth had been to destroy his credibility. It made no sense. Salim was a

Kelantanese, and he knew how angry people would get about such a bold-faced betrayal, whether it was Omar's jampi or Dris' feelings. Salim must have thought he was invulnerable.

Maryam was reminded how the most unlikely killers were suddenly discovered, when the most obvious and suspicious choice had done nothing. Maybe, she thought, she should look at the widows, as the least appealing candidates. If either of them killed Salim, their actions since had been a masterclass on nerves of steel. It was the kind of thing Maryam very much admired, and of course, she'd regret arresting anyone so clearly capable. Rather than be arrested, they should be taken into the army, for they could have given generals some lessons in sang-froid. She realized she was beginning to think like a fan rather than a detective, and sternly made herself move her thoughts in another direction.

Later that afternoon, when the day's heat was waning and it was marginally cooler than it had been, Sharifah arrived at her house, carrying with her a large papaya and a big smile.

'Mak Cik!' she called, and Maryam emerged from the house. She'd just returned from the market, and was beginning dinner, as was just about everyone else. It was an odd time to visit, since the guest would have to be invited to dinner, and it seemed presumptuous to present yourself. The Malay saying, *bawa perut kerumah orang,* to bring your stomach to someone else's house, covered just such a situation, in terms that clearly admonished people not to do it. Moreover, most people didn't like going out at the break of dawn or the fall of evening, when it was neither day nor night, and it was dark, but not quite. If one believed in ghosts and spirits, these were the times of day they were most likely to be out, and it was the perfect time to stay indoors, prepare dinner or say the Maghrib prayer.

And yet, there was Sharifah, looking pretty and bubbly and holding the papaya in front of her like a sword. 'Come up,' Maryam invited her, wiping her hands on a dishrag and wondering how she could continue with dinner preparations. However, hospitality came first, and Maryam dutifully produced cups of coffee and some cakes, and admired the papaya.

'From our garden,' Sharifah told her, smiling widely. Maryam made the appropriate noises of amazement and admiration, and while looking relaxed and delighted to welcome a visitor, counted the moments until Sharifah would state her business. She got to it fairly quickly.

'You know Mak Cik, I was thinking, I think I was rude when you came over the last time. I was busy, yes, but I was also tired of being asked questions, especially about my sister, who has nothing to do with any of this. And I should have acted without the proper respect to you and Mak Cik Rubiah, and I'm sorry.'

It was a lovely speech, and well delivered. Sharifah cast a demure glance down at her lap and then rose. 'It's so difficult for me to get away, with the children and all; this was the first moment I had when someone could watch them. I don't want to interrupt your dinner preparations. I just wanted to apologize. Thank you Mak Cik, and forgive the intrusion.'

'What intrusion?' Maryam cried, still holding the papaya. 'Won't you stay for dinner? It should be ready shortly.'

'No, thank you very much, I couldn't possibly. I've got to get home myself and make sure dinner is done.' She smiled. 'No thank you, but I do appreciate the offer. Another time, perhaps. Thank you!' She began backing out of the room and walking down the steps as Maryam continued to entice her to stay for dinner. She smiled and shook her head, wished Maryam a good night, and disappeared down the road.

She returned to the kitchen, and placed the papaya in the middle of the table. She berated herself for being crazily suspicious, but she wondered whether there was something in the fruit, and whether it had been brought to her as a warning. It looked like a fine specimen, but Maryam could not get out of her mind that it had been given to her to harm her, and so she refused to include it as dessert with dinner. She warned the family not to touch it, and decided to bring it to the police station the next morning, for what exactly she wasn't sure, but she didn't want it in the house.

In the morning, she felt like a fool, and wondered what had become of her when the gift of a papaya could terrify her. Fool or not, however, she didn't touch it, but brought it to Osman and explained where she'd gotten it.

'Do you think she might try to kill me with it?'

Osman looks doubtful. 'If she was, it was a bad way to go about it, since we'd all know who brought it to you.'

'I thought of that,' Maryam told him. 'But then I was afraid to eat it anyway. Maybe she doesn't care who knows it as long as she stops me.'

'It wouldn't stop anything,' Osman explained slowly. 'We know she brought it. If anything were to happen to you it isn't as if we'd leave her alone. You know, it may just be a papaya.'

'Do you want it?'

'No.' He told her. 'I'm afraid of it, though I don't think I should be.'

'See? It gets to you.'

Osman put it on a pile of papers in the corner of his desk. 'Forget about it. It's over. Now, what were you saying?'

'She specifically said her sister had nothing to do with it, but that would make me more suspicious of her. Could it be she was just apologizing?'

'Maybe,' Osman said. 'She and her sister spend a lot of time protecting each other.'

'Why even bring her up? I think that's odd. The whole thing just brought her and Bahiyah, and of course, the papaya, to our attention.

Rahman brought them both coffee, and prepared to leave the room. 'No, stay Man,' Osman urged him. 'You can help: we're talking about the case.'

Rahman smiled broadly to be invited into the highest levels of Kelantan detecting. He felt as if he'd finally arrived.

'You've heard about the papaya: a dangerous and frightening weapon.'

Rahman nodded.

'It's over there,' Osman pointed at it. Sitting on top of the papers, it looked quite innocuous. Just like a fruit, really.

'It isn't that frightening.'

'It just looks innocent,' Maryam said with a laugh. 'Don't let it fool you.'

'Sharifah brought it yesterday.' Rahman nodded. 'She came at dinnertime.' Rahman raised his eyebrows. 'Really. Did she stay?'

'I invited her, of course, but she said she had to get back and just came to apologize.'

'You don't hear that very often.' Rahman considered. 'It's nice that she did it, but it seems a little strange. Unless she felt her behaviour was unforgivable.'

'It wasn't that bad,' Maryam lit one of her cigarettes. Not the packaged kind, the market-woman kind you rolled yourself. 'I wasn't expecting to see her.'

'Mak Cik was wondering whether she was trying to lead attention away from someone.'

Rahman nodded. 'She didn't mention anyone?'

'Her sister.'

'Then …'

'But mentioning it only brought her to our attention, right?'

'Could it be it was only what it seemed to be?' Rahman asked. 'Just a gift of a papaya?'

'I'd hate to think I've been this worried about nothing,' Maryam said. 'I like to have a reason to be suspicious.'

Chapter XX

Maryam felt her increased vigilance had saved her and her family from possible harm, and made her careful about people in a way she had never been before. Upon returning to her market stall – because her kain songket wasn't going to sell itself – she noticed some notches in the wood of the platform. She called Rubiah down from her perch on the second floor of the market, and together they moved all the fabrics she had piled there in an order perhaps not immediately comprehensible to the uninitiated. Rubiah sifted through the folded silks and cottons, searching for something out of the ordinary, but found nothing. But the notches were definitely there and definitely new, and neither woman could understand what they were doing there.

'I wish I hadn't become so ... cautious,' Maryam told her, standing in front of her stall looking perplexed. 'Everything looks threatening to me. Even fruit.'

Rubiah nodded absently. Something about this made her uneasy. Someone took a good deal of time and trouble, in the middle of the night, because only then would the market be reliably empty, to make these careful notches, deep and numerous. They examined the lock, which held the planks closing the stall in place, and upon close inspection noticed scratches on it, and some on the plank it was on.

'Someone tried to break in,' Maryam said thoughtfully. 'Look at these scratches. I guess they couldn't take the time, or thought it was just too much trouble, and decided to do this instead. Do you think they were going to ruin my stock?' As a market woman, this was an attack on her very being. 'I can't believe this.' She turned to look at Rubiah, who was frowning at the cuts. 'What does this do? I can't figure it out.'

'It's a warning,' Rubiah said.

'I don't need a warning. I'm already warned. I won't even eat papaya.' She leaned over and rubbed her forefinger against the notches. 'Is there anything in these?' she wondered. She brought her finger away and examined it. There was nothing on it she could see, or feel. 'I don't understand.' She shook her head.

Rubiah needed to return to her own stall, and promised to see her after lunch, when the major crush for Malay cakes was over. Maryam carefully climbed up into her stall, looking around her for traps or weapons, but saw nothing else. It didn't mean she wasn't growing afraid.

Perhaps her unease communicated itself to her potential customers, because she got relatively few that morning, and the market itself was crowded. She tried to regulate the expression on her face, to eliminate worry and fear, and radiate good humour and confidence. It appeared to be working, she thought, a few more women stopped and laid coveting palms on the kain songket, opened the folded batik sarong, and two or three even bought something. She began to think about her business, and to brood less on threats, real or imagined.

A man came up to her stall, which was noteworthy in itself, for men were rarely buyers. He was an older man, a little stooped, dressed traditionally in a plaid sarong and white T-shirt. His grey hair was tucked under a head cloth, and he sported a particularly spotty grey beard, or rather a collection of long grey hairs sprouting from his chin. He reached over to the pile of cotton sarong, and rubbed the fabric between his thumb and forefinger. He smiled at her, minus a few teeth, and Maryam became immediately anxious.

'You don't know me,' he reported accurately. 'And I don't know you.' She shrank back against the wall and wished Rubiah would appear. 'But I've been sent here to tell you you're on the wrong track.'

'Who sent you to tell me that?'

He cackled an old man's laugh. 'I don't even know myself. But I can tell you: if I were you, I would take care of my family. Children, grandchildren. You should be protecting them.' Maryam went cold. Did they know about her new grandchildren-to-be? Were they looking at Nuraini and Zakaria, and her daughters and sons? It was intolerable.

He reached under the pile of batik and pulled out something black and broken, and she recognized the body of a large black spider, and instinctively pulled away from it. He had known just where to look, or had he brought it with him and put it there while she looked at his face? Maryam did not like spiders, which could become a problem in Kelantan, where they were both large and plentiful, but she could usually keep her distaste hidden. He grinned as he held it in front of her; Maryam thought she would scream or faint, either one a victory for him.

How did he, or they, know she hated these creatures? She never spoke of it – spiders were actually thought praiseworthy in Islam, since they wove webs over the cave in which Muhammad was hiding when he fled his enemies. Many Kelantanese refused to kill spiders in gratitude for their help, but Maryam would kill them if she felt provoked, which was any time she saw them. She dragged her eyes away: afraid to look, afraid not to look, and this was a dead one!

Suddenly the bile rose in her throat, and, instinctively protecting her inventory, she turned and vomited on him. She was actually aiming for the floor, she explained later, but missed it and hit him. Perhaps it was preferable, since she was spared cleaning the floor, and he jumped back and ran from the market, clutching the dead spider in his hand. Maryam tried to scramble down from the stall, but had a difficult time getting her legs to work, and was helped down by her friend in the next stall, clucking over the nerve of this man and setting Maryam gently on her feet. Both being cloth sellers, they immediately checked to make sure the fabrics were clean, and thank heaven, they were.

Maryam was helped up the stairs to Rubiah's stall, where she was cleaned up, given hot tea and a cold towel, and much concern. To their surprise, Osman showed up a few moments later, explaining one of his men had seen a vomit-covered old man outside the market, and heedless of his protests, brought him into the station. He had no clear explanation of how he became as begrimed as he was, and since he had come from the market, Osman thought he'd see if Maryam or Rubiah knew anything about it. He did not foresee they would know as much about it as they did.

Osman went downstairs immediately upon hearing what had happened, to examine the mysterious notches and look for any traces of poisons, weapons or evil spells. He found nothing, except the troubling and inexplicable notches. He could think of no reason for them, except as a warning, but even as that they were too vague to be really effective. He stood before the stall, rubbing the notches until he decided to look under the narrow shelf they were on. There, below them, he found dried blood with one or two small white feathers stuck to it. And a drawing of a spider, which had been rubbed in the blood, tucked into the joint of the wood. Osman examined it, front and back, but it seemed nothing remarkable, just the kind of picture a child would draw. He folded it and put it in his pocket.

Osman was relieved that he, and not Maryam, had found this. He hadn't been aware of her distaste for spiders, but didn't think it as singular as Maryam thought it was. He wasn't all that fond of them himself. Though he had held one as a child, it wasn't one of his favourite memories and could still bring a shudder. But did whoever left this know that about her (and if they did, how?) or was it a lucky guess that most people wouldn't want to be presented with one, dead or alive? He was inclined to the lucky guess theory but feared he liked it because it was the easiest way out and would require less effort from him. And whoever did it meant Maryam harm, there was no mistaking that, and might escalate to something that would really hurt her.

He brought her, together with Rubiah, who refused to leave

her, to the station to confront her attacker. No one had let him clean up, and he sat in the corner of the room still covered in vomit. Everyone stayed as far away as possible, but Rahman was adamant that no kindness be shown to him after what he'd done.

The man's name was Hatim, and he came from Cabang Tiga, just down the road from Kampong Banggol, ground zero for all their suspects. He complained loudly that he knew nothing about it, that he'd been hired to do what he did, that he didn't even know Maryam. She confirmed this, but it wasn't a surprise. Zul was zealously taking notes, though taking care to keep his distance.

'Do you know Pak Cik Omar? The bomoh from Kampong Banggol?' Zul asked suddenly, apropos of nothing. Hatim looked startled. Zul narrowed in. 'You do, don't you?' Zul disappeared into the cells, and returned holding Omar by the arm.

'Look who's here!' He said to Omar, whose jaw dropped and he began sputtering. 'Who's this? Filthy, disgusting, why …' He did not seem able to get out a full sentence.

'I threw up on him,' Maryam explained helpfully. 'Couldn't help it.'

Hatim sat there, his eyes darting from Omar to Zul to Maryam.

'We picked him up,' Zul informed Omar. 'He was in the street covered in … just like this. So of course, our police thought it was suspicious.' Oman tried to pull away from him but Zul wrenched him back. 'You sent him, didn't you?'

Omar said nothing, but regarded Hatim with disgust. 'If you knew what you looked like …'

'He knows,' Rahman said. 'He just can't do anything about it. So tell us, how do you know each other?'

They both looked sullen. 'I said it was the bomoh, didn't I?' Zul reminded Rahman. 'They understand this kind of thing. The rest of us don't even want to.'

Osman sat down at his desk and began arranging paper. 'You,' he directed his gaze at Omar, 'hired this poor old man to go to the market to try and frighten this mak cik, who works for the police. She's harder to frighten than you realize, so she protected herself by throwing up.'

This was a spin Maryam would never have invented: defensive vomiting. It made her sound like an adept at an exceptionally obscure martial art. And beyond that, she knew she wasn't that hard to frighten, she'd been terrified, but best not to say anything about it. Let her look like a warrior queen, working only with the weapons she had at hand.

'What is the blood under the shelf?' Osman asked. Maryam looked shocked. 'Did you put it there last night?' He turned to Hatim, who now looked confused. 'It was him, wasn't it?' he asked Omar. Not waiting for an answer, or not interested in one, he continued. 'What was the point here? To frighten Mak Cik Maryam into leaving the investigation? You don't know who you're dealing with: she'd never abandon a case because of intimidation.'

Osman glared at them both. 'You're quite a pair, the two of you. Look at you.' He shook his head in disgust. 'Put them both in the cells.' Zul grabbed them both and pushed them to the other room.

'Zul's really coming along, isn't he?' Rahman commented.

'He reminds me of you,' Osman told him, grinning.

Rahman smiled back. 'It was good thinking to put them together. Maybe they'll talk.'

'Or gag,' Osman answered.

'What kind of luck was that, finding him right away? Otherwise he would have disappeared and we wouldn't know anything about him.'

'Quick thinking, Mak Cik,' Rahman congratulated her. 'Marking him like that so we couldn't miss him.'

'Yes, I planned it. By the way, where's the papaya?' Maryam asked, looking around the room for it.

'Oh, sorry, Mak Cik,' one of the policeman said. 'Were we supposed to keep it for you?'

'No,' Maryam began.

'We ate it. Great papaya,' he assured her.

She gave Osman a rueful look.

Chapter XXI

'So,' she was telling her story to Mamat, 'Osman made it sound like I used my secret weapon of throwing up to save myself.'

Mamat laughed delightedly. 'I love that! It makes you sound so fierce. And it's so much better than saying you did it from fear.'

'I agree, but Mamat, how did Omar know I'd be afraid of … them.' She didn't even like saying the word. It made her uneasy. 'That's what makes me nervous.'

'No, it's nothing. Think about what most people are afraid of: spiders and snakes. He could have chosen either.'

'Yes, but he didn't. He *knew*.'

Mamat lost his happy expression. 'How? We never talk about it.'

'That's just it.' She rose from the couch and began pacing the living room. 'There's no reason to guess. You know a lot of people feel thankful, I don't know if that's the right word, to them and wouldn't mind looking at them.'

'At a dead one?'

Maryam shuddered. She was having a hard time getting that picture out of her mind. 'Maybe.'

'I'll go with you to the market tomorrow,' Mamat decided.

'Just to make sure nothing happens.'

'Can you check the stall first, before I go into it? What if he left one there?' Her voice began to take on a higher pitch.

'I'm sure he didn't,' he soothed her. 'And anyway, I'll check.'

* * *

He was as good as his word. While Maryam lingered next to their motorbike, pretending to be deeply engrossed in the fish market, Mamat went to her stall, unlocked it and took down the slats covering it. He examined the back and the front of each board, and saw nothing out of the usual. He put them away, and felt under the shelf, feeling it sticky. Pulling his hands away, he saw they were stained with the blood Osman had found yesterday, and he went to find some water to wash – he couldn't possibly search the fabrics with dirty hands. He came back with wet rag and scrubbed vigorously at the wood, removing every trace of blood he could find: he did not want Maryam feeling it, and reliving the whole episode again.

Methodically, Mamat took every pile of fabric and moved it, searched under it, and unfolded each piece. He carefully put them back in the same order he'd found them, for Maryam was very particular about being able to put her hands immediately on any piece of fabric in the stall.

He found nothing else in his search, and prepared to get Maryam when he glanced up at the top of the stall. It had a roof of sorts: plywood boards nailed together to keep out any particularly acrobatic thief, and in the corner, he thought he saw something. He climbed onto the platform, noting the cryptic notches there, and reached to find what it was, when another black spider corpse fell, landing on his shoulder. He leapt off the platform while frantically slapping at his shoulder, and very nearly broke his leg in the process. And he wasn't even afraid of them, but neither did he want one on his shirt. He kept whirling around, checking his shoulder, his shirt, his legs and the floor, turning cold and clammy and wanting to cry.

He saw it, finally, crushed on the floor where he must have stamped on it in his mad frenzy. He was breathing hard; other market women were looking at him warily, and he held on to the stall to keep from falling. After a few moments, when he could trust himself to stand and his heart no longer felt like it was coming out of his chest, he cleaned the floor and checked the stall again, making doubly sure this time there was nothing for Maryam to find.

Smoothing back his hair and taking deep, cleansing breaths, he walk out to bring Maryam in. She took one look at him and retreated. 'What happened?' she asked.

'Nothing,' he tried to smile and look nonchalant, but even while he was doing it he knew he was failing.

'You found another one.' She was now white with terror.

'No,' he lied unconvincingly. 'No, I just slipped getting down. It's perfectly safe. I've checked everything. I promise.'

'Who is doing this to me? Why?' She wrung her hands, which Mamat had almost never seen her do.

'Come,' he put his arm around her shoulder and led her into the market. 'I'll stay here and make sure nothing happens.'

He spent the day on a folding chair in front of her stall, drinking endless cups of coffee and smoking unceasingly, taking the occasional break to eat some cake. He looked indolent, but kept a sharp watch on Maryam, and held his breath every time she unfolded a fabric, even though he'd already checked. He feared another would just materialize out of nowhere to scare her.

She glanced at him occasionally, as if drawing moral support from his presence, but in general, kept her mind on her work. Mamat admired that about her, how determined she could be, and how diligent. He thought himself diligent as well, but freely admitted he was not in her league. He could be distracted, and become thirsty or hungry or crave a cigarette, but she on the other hand was capable of shutting all that out if she wanted to accomplish something. And her stall was crucial to their income and to her vision of herself, and she would not be frightened away from working. But, Mamat thought, he might be sitting in this chair for several days.

Chapter XXII

Dris looked tired lately, and he seemed to have lost all joy in living. Nik Man had come to talk to him about their next tournament, taking care not to approach the topic of love or attachment, but even seeing him did not cheer up Dris. Latifah watched him carefully, but did not intervene; while she wasn't angry, exactly, neither was she filled with concern. Dris nearly brought ruin on them all, and even now it was still possible, though she hoped the interest would simply dissipate as Salim began to fade into memory. She continued her daily rounds, took care of the children and put a plate in front of her husband at dinnertime, but did not inquire into his state of mind.

Dris moped off to his rice land in the early morning, and came back in the early afternoon, when the sun was at its hottest. At home, he was withdrawn, and did not go out, as had been his wont; certainly, he did not go to Nik Man's house. He sat on the porch most of the time, smoking cigarettes and staring down at the floor, while his children ran around him, treating him like a movable piece of furniture.

And then, one day, he was gone. He left in the morning to go to his padi field, or so Latifah assumed, but when he hadn't returned by sundown, she became concerned, and walked out to the field herself with her two eldest children to try to find him. They called out for him, walked the dikes in the field, which wasn't all that large, so it took little time to cover it completely, but found no trace of him. He'd obviously been working the field: it was well tended and neat. But he wasn't there.

Latifah returned to the house and sent her son to call the police. When Osman arrived, she was cleaning up the dinner dishes, and was, as he had seen her before, utterly composed.

'I thought you should know,' she told him. 'He's a suspect and all that, so he's disappeared, that's a problem, isn't it? I don't know where he went or why,' she forestalled the next question. 'He's been very strange the last week or so, not talking to anyone, just sitting on the porch staring. He hasn't even spoken to Nik Man – though I don't think he can go over to their house anymore, Sharifah would never let him in. Nik Man was here once, talking to him about the next contest coming up, but Dris didn't even talk much then.'

'I'm not surprised he was depressed,' Osman began slowly. 'Where would he most likely have gone? His parents? Brothers and sisters?'

She shook her head. 'His parents are gone. His brother is in Kampong Sabak, just down the coast, but they aren't all that close.'

'Still, it's the most obvious place to look,' Osman said, rising to his feet. Give me his name and where his house is. I'm going to look there – maybe his brother knows something.'

Latifah looked doubtful, but dutifully provided him with the information, and watched him go, calmly, as she did everything.

* * *

Osman and Rahman arrived in Kampong Sabak. It was now full night, after dinner. There was a shadow play performance going on in the next village and many people were already there. However, Dris' brother Arifin was not a fan, though his wife and children had gone; he was sitting in his living room watching television and enjoying the quiet. He was surprised to see two policemen at the bottom of his steps, but invited them up nevertheless and then looked around helplessly for coffee and snacks.

'My wife has gone to see the performance,' he waved his hand vaguely in that direction, 'and I don't have, that is, I don't know …'

'Don't trouble yourself,' Osman assured him. 'We're fine. We just have a few questions for you.'

'Me?' he squeaked.

'No, you haven't done anything. It's about your brother, Dris.'

Arifin relaxed noticeably. 'Oh. Dris.'

'Yes, he seems to have disappeared?'

Arifin regarded them quizzically. 'Really?'

'Yes. Have you heard about the murder at the kite flying contest?'

He nodded. 'Of course.'

'Yes, well, Dris was a suspect.'

'I heard.'

'Did he tell you?'

'Sort of. Latifah told me.'

'Well, he seemed quite depressed about it.'

'Do you think he did it?'

'I don't know yet. But there were a few people who might have …'

'I heard that too. Omar and Nik Man and Halimah, and oh, I know there were more.'

'Right.'

'And you thought Dris might have killed him. Latifah said Salim blackmailed him; though can you call it blackmail if he told everyone about it and wasn't looking to be paid? But just to spread these rumours.'

'Yes, that's it.'

'Only not really rumours, as I understand it.' He looked keenly at Osman.

Osman cleared his throat. 'Not totally rumours, I don't think. Did you ever discuss that with your brother?'

'It would be hard to do, wouldn't it?' Arifin fixed his gaze on the far wall. 'I thought Dris might have felt something … I don't know … different, for Nik Man. The way he followed him around. The way he talked about him. And the way he got so mad if you criticized him at all. You might say I knew something but I didn't want to know. That's the truth.'

'I'm sure it is.'

'But it made his life very difficult, you see. I noticed that. Latifah is a wonderful woman, and she pretended not to see anything, but their marriage wasn't what it should have been. I blame Dris for that.'

'Maybe he couldn't help it.'

'I'm sure he couldn't. I don't think he would have chosen it, if it were up to him. But there it is.' He offered cigarettes, which he had to hand, in lieu of coffee and cakes, but it was more than sufficient. They all lit up.

'Where do you think he would have gone to?' Osman asked him.

Arifin shook his head. 'I have no idea, really. None at all. I mean, he didn't come here and that would be the logical place, you know. I don't think he has lots of close friends, aside from Nik Man, and I can't imagine he'd go there. No, I can't think of anywhere else.'

'He can't have just gone. He has to be somewhere.'

'Maybe.' Arifin thought. 'You don't think he might have done himself harm?' he asked, looking a bit concerned. 'Could he have decided he couldn't bear it anymore?' Now he no longer seemed only vaguely interested.

Osman considered it. 'I don't like to think that.'

'Did you look in his field? He was probably getting it ready for the next planting.'

'Latifah said she'd looked there. It's dark now; I thought we'd look first thing in the morning when we could see. She might have missed something.'

Arifin nodded. 'I'll meet you at the field in the morning.'

* * *

At first light, the Kota Bharu police department was out in full force, gathered at a small rice field inland from the coast at Pantai Cinta Berahi. It was, as Latifah had noted, well-cared-for, though still dry, as the planting season had not yet begun. They walked the dikes, as Latifah had done the day before, and peered at the dry soil to see if they could find any footprints, but the soil was hard, and showed nothing. The land bordered on a coconut grove, with some brush at the border of the two. Osman walked the border, kicking at the grass, and kicked up an undamaged pack of cigarettes, caught amid the blades. He bent down and picked it up, brushing it off, though it was really still clean. Mild Seven brand. He held it up to Rahman. 'Could this be Dris'? Is this what he smoked?' Rahman shrugged but Arifin came over to examine it.

'This is his brand. But it could be anyone's cigarettes.'

'I know,' Osman replied, wrapping it in his handkerchief, as he had seen done on television, though Kota Bharu had no way of testing for fingerprints. It was the process of being professional, he thought, and not always a question of what kind of facilities you had.

They looked all the harder in the area where the cigarettes were found, but there was nothing there. Osman felt something was wrong, that he was missing something, that Dris needed to be found quickly in order to avoid a tragedy, but aside from this premonition, he could find no solid evidence.

'Could he have gone away to think?' Zul asked.

'Think about what,' Arifin answered. 'What did he have to think about which would make him leave home?' Zul had no answer to this, but simply frowned at the dry, unrevealing earth.

He really wanted to solve this, but had no idea how to continue from here. 'Do you think he might have been killed?' he whispered to Rahman, who shrugged and said nothing. 'Do you think he might have killed himself?' Zul asked again, and Rahman turned to him. 'I hope not,' he said. 'That would be so sad.' Zul nodded, but did not discard the notion.

Osman motioned for them to spread out, and look in the neighbouring fields. The sun was higher now, and it was becoming hotter. The rice fields offered no protection from the sun, and the coconut grove offered only minimal shade, which one had to leave in order to scour the ground. Rahman was getting very hot and very thirsty, but was determined not to be the first to request a halt. He'd keep looking until he was told not to, and he'd ignore the heat. He wandered farther through the coconut palms, which were his favourite kind of tree: so tall and graceful, with feathery leaves waving at every breeze. He looked up to admire a particularly tall tree, and incidentally, to stand in its shade for a moment. Something caught his eye at the end of the grove, almost into the rice field on the other side. He walked briskly to it, and bent down to find a man's sarong lying in a heap. Men in Kelantan wore plaid cotton sarong, called *kain pelikat*, and frankly one plaid sarong was much like another unless it used an unusual colour, like purple, instead of the common blues and greens. This sarong though, was garden variety: it was neither new nor worn, neither sparkling clean nor noticeably dirty, and it was the plaid of a thousand other sarong all over Kelantan.

He called to Osman, who came over with Arifin to examine the find. 'Is this his?' Rahman asked. Arifin looked baffled.

'I don't know. It looks like any sarong, doesn't it? It could be anyone's.' He looked at it more closely but he was correct: it had no identifying marks, and looked like every other sarong worn by every other man. Osman sighed, picked up a stick and drove it into the ground at the spot where Rahman found it. He doubted it mattered, really, but once more reminded himself about professional process. He looked around the field and ordered the search to spread out even more, encompassing more of the neighbouring land, advising everyone to look for any kind of clue, even cigarette butts.

There were plenty of those, of various brands and of various ages, and Osman doubted any of them would be of the slightest help. But he thought of Latifah and her children, and felt he owed it to them, and to Dris himself, to find a coherent story about what happened to Dris. If anything at all happened to him – what if he only decided to leave this whole mess behind and go … where? With no money, and no relatives other than those here looking for him, there didn't seem to be many places for Dris to go. And that worried Osman, for with nowhere to go, he was probably close by, and if he hadn't been alerted to the monumental noise they were making, then he probably couldn't hear.

Two hours later, when the search party, born and bred in Kelantan heat, looked wilted to a worrying degree, Osman called a halt. They'd found cigarettes aplenty, an untouched box of Mild Sevens, an unidentified man's sarong and not much else. It was disheartening, and he also feared heatstroke, if not in his men then certainly in himself. They needed shade and water, and they trooped back to the main road and commandeered the small coffee stall, making the owner's income for several weeks. They were a quiet crew, deep in thoughts of where Dris could be, uneasy that they couldn't find him, and a bit guilty too, at the thought of returning to his wife with nothing to report.

Rahman leaned back on his stool (not too far back, which would land him on his back) and surveyed the fields they'd just come from, which they'd examined as he believed no field had been examined before. Something caught his attention, and he put his hand on Osman's arm. 'What?' asked Osman, looking in the direction Rahman indicated. He saw nothing he hadn't seen all morning, rice fields awaiting the rains, coconut groves and a field of tobacco plants. Rahman pointed to a field beyond the tobacco, browner than the rest but otherwise unremarkable. 'What?' he repeated.

Rahman rose from his stool, still staring into the distance. 'Do you see that field?' he asked in a preoccupied way. 'It's too brown.'

'What?' Osman was getting tired of hearing himself say it.

'It's too brown,' he repeated. 'It's mud. There aren't muddy fields right now.'

'Maybe they're getting it ready for planting.' Rahman shook his head. Osman stood up and stared. 'Maybe they flooded it for the water buffalo.'

'Yes. Why though?'

'What are you thinking?'

'I'm thinking maybe Dris is in there under the kerbau. Who'd look there? And the kerbau would be wallowing and it all seems quite normal, but …'

Osman signalled his troops to get up. They gulped the rest of their drinks and in a willing yet depleted spirit followed him to the field where indeed, a kerbau was relaxing up to its nose in mud, and in no mood to move. Rahman could sympathize, and in fact, the mud did look cool and inviting, so he plunged in, ostensibly to coax out the kerbau, but also just to feel the blessed moisture around him. He'd get another uniform, he was doing this for his job.

Zul waded in behind him. They were both kampong boys, and knew a thing or two about persuading reluctant buffalos to get up and move. In the spirit of the men around him, the kerbau, with an easily readable look of resignation on his face, hauled himself to his feet and allowed himself to be led to the edge of his wallow. Rahman knew the buffalo's patience was not infinite, and they needed to look quickly before the beast reclaimed his wallow and knocked them into it. As the animal stood, shifting his weight from one foot to another and snorting in a comradely sort of way, Rahman, Zul and two of the other policemen bent into the mud and felt around, there being no more scientific way to look for anything. The mud was not as deep as these things usually were, probably because it was the dry season and someone had to actually get the water over here, but they stamped and leaned over and felt something, and all four of them leaned in and yanked as hard as they could. With a loud sucking sound, Dris was pulled from the mud, quite dead and quite trampled. They brought him to dry land, and the kerbau, seeing them leave his dominion, immediately threw himself back into the mud and resumed his spot with only his eyes and nose sticking out. They wouldn't bother him a second time.

Chapter XXIII

Standing around the same coffee stall, having poured bucket after bucket of water over Dris to clean him off, they looked at him sadly. Lying at the bottom of a buffalo wallow could destroy a body, and Dris' was bruised and broken, but Osman despaired of ever knowing whether he'd entered the mud dead or alive. Or jumped in himself or was thrown. Any clues were now encased in mud and guarded by a buffalo, and that's assuming any clues existed.

Rahman sighed, so sorry for Dris and this end. 'Do you think he did it to himself?' Zul asked. 'To kill himself, I mean.'

'I know, but I don't know. How will we ever? Look at that body, poor thing. If you want to kill yourself, that's a very tough way to do it,' he meditated. 'It's like drowning and being beaten at the same time.'

'Poor kerbau,' Zul said unexpectedly. 'It's unfair to make the kerbau kill you. He's just an innocent animal.'

Rahman looked at him in surprise. 'You know, I was thinking the same thing, but thought people would think I was crazy myself to say it.'

'Not me,' Zul assured him. 'Don' worry.'

Osman walked up to them, 'I'm going to tell Latifah.'

'I'll come with you,' Rahman volunteered. 'Don't go alone.' He looked down at himself, now as muddy as any buffalo. 'Um, I'll stand at the bottom of the stairs,' he allowed. 'I'm not fit for human company.'

Osman suddenly flashed a smile. 'No, you stay outside with the geese.'

* * *

Latifah took the news with the same placidity that she'd shown when confronted with anything they'd told her. 'I was afraid of this,' she said quietly, looking down from the porch at Rahman. 'You're a mess.'

'Yes, Mak Cik.'

'He went into the mud to take out the ... Dris.'

'Thank you,' she told him. 'I didn't mean to embarrass you.'

'No, Mak Cik. I am a mess, you're right.'

'You can bathe at the well and I'll lend you some clothes, if you'd like. I'm grateful for what you've done ...' Anything else she said disappeared into the house, and she emerged a moment later with a sarong, pants, shirt and a towel. 'The well's there,' she pointed.

While Rahman cleaned up, immensely relieved to clean off the mud encasing him like armour, Latifah brought tea and cigarettes for them all. 'Do you think he was killed?' she asked Osman, 'or do you think he killed himself? I'm sure the kerbau had nothing to do with it.'

Osman was a city boy himself, from Ipoh, Perak, and did not have the same feelings towards water buffalo that he'd heard this morning from everyone who'd mentioned it. Everyone, from Rahman to Zul to Latifah made sure to comment on the kerbau's innocence in all this, as though they feared he might bring the animal in for questioning. He thought it endearing, all this concern for the beast and its feelings, and the way even the widow launched a pre-emptive defence.

'The kerbau is not a suspect in any way,' he assured her. 'He is free to go about his business.'

She smiled. 'I'm glad someone's been ruled out.'

'Do you think your husband was in a state of mind where he might have harmed himself?'

'Possibly. He was very unlike himself. Quiet and withdrawn, not talking to anyone, not going anywhere. You know,' she took a drag on her cigarette and looked hard at it, 'I think I may be to blame a little.

'I could see he was unhappy. I saw him dragging himself around, but I didn't ask him about anything. I was fed up,' she admitted calmly, 'I thought we'd all suffered enough because of him and I didn't want to hear anymore about how he was feeling. What about me? And the kids? He never asked about us, so I thought I'm not asking about him. I was wrong, I guess. I should have been nicer.'

'You've been through a lot,' Osman assured her sympathetically.

'We all have. Well, maybe I should have asked him. It's too late now.' She sipped her tea. 'Who would have killed him? If Dris knew who the killer was, maybe that was the reason.'

'Do you think he did?'

'I don't think Dris killed Salim, anyway. If it were Nik Man, and Dris knew it, would he tell anyone?' She thought about it. 'No, he wouldn't. He'd die first.' She thought about what she'd just said. 'Maybe he did.' She sighed.

'Will you be alright?' Osman asked, concerned. 'Do you have enough for the kids and you ...'

She waved her hand, dismissing his worry. 'I made most of the money,' she smiled, this was Kelantan, after all. 'And we'll have his rice field. I'll rent it out. I have brothers and sisters, I'll be fine. I'll miss him, you know. He wasn't the best husband: I wish I'd known about all that before I married him. But anyway, he's gone and I'm sorry. I hope he didn't kill himself ...'

'As do I,' Osman agreed, but from a police standpoint, he wasn't sure what was preferable. Rahman walked onto the porch, clean, his hair still wet and his uniform rolled into a bundle.

'You'll never get that clean,' Latifah advised him.

'I know,' he answered.

'We'll give you another one,' Osman assured him. 'Done in the line of duty.'

Rahman smiled sadly and sat down next to them, thanking Latifah.

'I'm so sorry,' he said.

'We were just talking about it,' she said quietly. 'I have to tell the children.' She sighed. 'I hate to do it, but they must know. It's so sad to lose a father.'

She rose. 'Thank you for coming to tell me. I'm afraid I can't talk right now.'

They left, Rahman still clutching his filthy uniform, which his mother tried to clean several times, and then decided to burn it, as she told herself she should have right at the beginning.

Chapter XXIV

Rahman was called in to give his opinion on wedding decorations and the colour scheme. As Mamat had advised Azmi, and as Malay fathers had advised their sons for decades, Rahman's father advised him. 'Say you like everything and agree with whatever she says on this,' he told him. 'Do you really care about wedding decorations? Of course not. Don't start a fight. Just agree.'

This had been his plan all along, so it was not difficult to internalize. Aliza showed him the white songket being made into her dress, and the white songket he would wear as a waistcloth and headdress. He agreed with enthusiasm. He admired the decorations being readied by Ashikin and her minions, and the chairs they would sit on 'in state'. He was the perfect groom. Mamat caught his eye while they were looking at fabric and gave him an approving smile and nod, and Rahman was proud to have done his job so well.

The wedding was only two weeks away, and Aliza was perfectly composed. Ashikin was getting a bit testy, being in charge of the decorations and also feeling her pregnancy, but no one could deprive her of her authority. Maryam walked around beaming at the thought of the wedding. Yi's appearance: tall for his age, gangly and occasionally frightening when walking near breakable objects, was the despair of his female relatives. There was no hope for it, and Aliza was heard to comment to her mother, 'Do you still think he's improving? Are you sure you aren't blinded by mother love? Azmi never looked like this.' Maryam gave her a stern look, but did think that indeed, Azmi never looked this gawky. However, as his mother, it was up to her to stay optimistic about Yi's growing out of this awkward stage, and resolved to stay the course.

Rubiah had been baking for the wedding, determined to keep up the highest standards. Even Daud, Ashikin's husband, and Azmi had been roped in by their wives to hang decorations and carry large objects. After all, both their wives were pregnant and prone to back pain, and also impatience. Only Mamat and Abdullah, Rubiah's husband, stayed out of the fray, smiling at everyone, committing to nothing, looking pleased at all they saw.

Maryam remembered her discussion with Ashikin and their hope to have this case finished by the wedding, but Maryam felt she was at an impasse. Everyone seemed so very calm about everything. At Dris' funeral, Latifah conducted herself with gravity and control, and even her children seemed muted, but courteous. Nik Man looked pained, and spoke of how Dris had been one of his closest friends and his helper, but Maryam thought he was trying to look unaffected, to avoid raking up any scandal about Dris again. Sharifah was silent and expressionless, and Omar was not in attendance, still in jail. Malay funerals were for the most part extremely restrained affairs to someone more used to

Western norms, and it was bad form to cry and even worse to make a fuss. Dignity and decorum were the watchwords, and all who attended lived up to the ideal.

The general consensus, as publicly discussed, was that Dris' death was an accident, an act of God, and inexplicable piece of ill fortune. No one wanted to say Dris killed himself, with all the religious disapproval that would cause, and no one wanted to say anyone else killed him either, at least not at the funeral. The odd conditions of his death allowed the cause to remain vague. To Osman's amusement, several people commented on the blamelessness of the kerbau, who could not be held responsible in any way. Osman gravely assured them the buffalo was under no suspicion, and would not even be questioned.

Osman, however, believed it was murder rather than suicide, though he couldn't prove it yet. He felt that Dris' malaise of the last days of his life would only have made the murder easier, as Dris was in no mood to fight off any attack, and might have even welcomed it as a way out of all his troubles. At least Omar was out of the running as a possible murderer, since they knew exactly where he was, so it left Nik Man, Sharifah and her family, and Halimah as possible suspects. He doubted Halimah, who seemed to have no further interest in the crime or in its aftereffects, though if it were her, she'd be a particularly cunning sort of criminal.

Even though the papaya turned out just to be a particularly lovely specimen of the fruit, Sharifah remained suspicious to Osman. Stopping by to apologize seemed a bit over the top, and Osman somehow felt Sharifah was behind a lot of what Nik Man did. He wished he could clarify his thoughts on this rather than simply feeling something was up, which wasn't all that helpful in terms of action.

* * *

In the morning, Mamat went out as he always did to feed his birds as the sun rose, before the morning heat might ruin their appetites. He mashed bananas and papaya (for vitamins) and ground some nuts, which he added merely for piquancy, so the birds wouldn't get bored with what they ate.

Stepping out on the porch, he found a small cage next to one of his large ones, and in it, a young merbok, already chirping and looking at him with that sweet yet impudent look the best birds had. He looked around, but the yard was deserted, the kampong still quiet. He understood immediately this was restitution for his killed bird, which still didn't ease the pain of what his dove had gone through when the poor thing had been hung. Mamat could still not bear to think about it, and maybe never would be able to.

Nevertheless, this was an excellent bird, a future champion, and someone had gone to a great deal of trouble in choosing it. It was hard to reconcile the same person (as he had no doubt it was) had both hung an innocent dove, and then chosen such a lovely substitute. He brought the bird out and let it sit in his hands. It sang a few notes, then chirped to itself, then watched Mamat with its black eyes and Mamat fell in love.

* * *

Omar still sat in his cell, thinking dark thoughts about everything that landed him here, including Hatim, a fool who had finally been able to wash and change out of his disgusting clothes. Hatim tried to talk to Omar, about what, Omar had no idea since he cut him off immediately whenever he opened his mouth. What he'd asked Hatim to do was so simple, so quick; it was mindboggling how he had managed to get arrested doing it. And to be vomited on, which was amazing in its own right. Omar cursed himself for getting involved in any of this, and for ever speaking to Salim, which was the seminal act that led to all of this.

Omar wanted nothing more than for things to go back to what they were before, so his life, which he had quite liked, could continue. Now, even if he were to be freed and exonerated, nothing would be the same, and nothing would be as good. And in the meantime, his entire business was leaching away as he sat here, unable to do anything, while the rest of the world went about its business leaving him behind. As people said: *yang rebah ditindeh:* he who falls is then stepped on.

He wondered whether Nik Man was still going to kite flying contests (the answer was yes), and what he would do without his assistant. He worried about who Nik Man was using for his jampi – he could get no information in jail and Nik Man certainly wasn't coming to visit him. He worried about whether he would be condemned for Salim's murder and forced to suffer for it, though he believed he had already suffered enough just being in jail. Being incarcerated for life or close to it was unthinkable – and he wasn't even in the main jail in Kelantan, just in the police holding cells. It was too horrible to contemplate.

When he learned of Dris' death, he was terrified. He felt as if the judgment of heaven was now coming down, and no one would be spared its vengeance. He didn't know whether Dris had been killed or killed himself, but he did not even pause to consider the theory of accident. Once you were close enough to a buffalo wallow to fall in, it was already no accident. As this was not Dris' kerbau, there was no reason for him to be that close to it for any reason. Omar believed it far too suggestive that a suspect in a murder also happened to be strolling around unrelated water buffalos and falling into the mud under their feet. He understood completely why mourners at his funeral might prefer that theory to any other, but as one who was removed from the situation, he didn't have to perform the mental contortions necessary to believe it.

He wondered whether it was Nik Man who killed him, perhaps because of the humiliation he bore after Salim told everyone. And if it were Nik Man, would Nik Man then come for him? Omar always thought of Nik Man as a nice man, a family man interested in his kites and his children and his wife. But if he started killing, even his oldest friend, what hope would there be for him when he was finally set free from this wretched place? Was he to go from jail to Nik Man's vengeance? He'd never thought of Nik Man in this light, but regarding it all from his shadowy cell, Nik Man assumed the proportions of a born killer, a cold blooded avenger, a man who would never let the slight of his working for Salim go without punishment. Without anyone else saying a word to him, Omar managed to terrify himself, and see death coming for him on an unswerving path. He shuddered in his cell and let waves of self-pity wash over him. It simply wasn't fair that a monster like Nik Man should hunt him, Omar, an innocuous bomoh without a particle of ill will towards anyone. There was no justice.

Chapter XXV

Sharifah went to Bahiyah's house with the children, to do nothing in particular except feel the comfort of being with her sister at a difficult time. They did not discuss Dris, either his life or his death, nor how he had felt about Nik Man, nor what Latifah was likely to do now that she was the sole support of the family. They discussed recipes their mother had perfected for fish curry, and debated which brand of Kelantan curry powder might be considered the best. Sharifah leaned back against the wall on her sister's porch, while her sister spoke softly about cooking and occasionally stroked her little sister's hair. Maryam would never have recognized this Bahiyah, warm and nurturing, quiet and soothing. If she were able to see her as she was with Sharifah and her nieces and nephews, it would explain a great deal about her status in Sharifah's life.

With her return to Bahiyah, Sharifah returned to her childhood, where she was protected, pampered as the youngest. She'd been fussed over by Bahiyah who brought her up: she was Bahiyah's first child to raise, and she retained her status even into adulthood. And while adulthood, by and large, went quite well, right now Sharifah was confused and an anxious, longing to return to the safety of her younger years.

She had never expected things to get so complicated. She'd never really thought about Dris, beyond remarking that he seemed to stay a boy admiring Nik Man. Salim's nasty tales opened her eyes to Dris, and she felt as though she was first noticing him. Nik Man's reaction revealed to her that he'd known all along, and, she suspected, had used it to keep Dris useful to him. Her husband vehemently denied he returned Dris' affection, or that it had ever been overtly recognized, but Sharifah, who'd spent a good deal of time in the past weeks thinking about it, didn't believe that. She was willing enough to accept that Nik Man did return Dris' regard; in fact, she was positive about it. But blind to it? Not at all.

Sharifah also knew the gossip about Dris would affect their family; it was impossible that it would leave them untouched. People would look at Nik Man and wonder what had gone on all those years, and look at Sharifah and wonder what she knew as well. The fact that she knew nothing would be immediately discarded, it was not the stuff of stirring gossip. Instead it would be embroidered and embellished, and people would look at her and raise their eyebrows, and her children would be teased at school. With Dris dead, she could only hope the gossip would concentrate on his death rather than his life, and leave her family alone.

She looked over at her older sister, who was smiling at her fondly. 'What are you thinking about so deeply?' she asked her.

'About Dris.'

Bahiyah tightened her lips.

'Do you think people will talk about Dris and us? Or do you think it will all change now that he's dead and people will just gossip about him dying in a buffalo wallow?'

'People forget,' Bahiyah soothed her. 'After all, it isn't really Nik Man they're talking about.'

'Do you think so?' Sharifah sat up and looked at her. 'I don't want them to say Nik Man and Dris … I don't want them saying anything to my kids at school. Or to me, and pity me like they pity Latifah.'

'How could they? Look at you and Nik Man. People envy your marriage, so happy, so strong. No one could think that about either of you,' she insisted stoutly. 'Latifah's been in that situation for so long and there's been some talk, but really, no one cared. If they didn't care about that they certainly can't care about you!

'Besides,' she lowered her voice so no one could hear her except Sharifah, 'it's really a good thing Dris has passed. Don't say it,' she held up her hand, 'I'm not celebrating at a death, and I'm sorry he's dead and sorry for Latifah and the children. But with him gone there will be no more talk in a month or two. You'll see.'

* * *

Halimah stayed in the house she lived in with Salim, just as she had said she would. She had the land she'd worked so hard to get, and had registered it in her name with those of her children, and felt she'd really accomplished something for them. It gave them a good start, she thought, a little more money than she'd ever received from her own parents, and it had been her ambition to give her children all that she could. She'd think about right before she fell asleep and it would lift her spirits. She'd succeeded.

Her children, particularly her daughter, thought it had been too much for her to do for them, and she'd suffered in a way her daughter would never have wanted for her mother. She was grateful her mother worried about her as she did, and worked so hard for them, but had hated Salim and how he treated her. She was glad he was dead: yes, she'd admit it to anyone. And she was even happier her mother was finally free of him.

It was odd, Halimah reflected, that once she'd gotten the land, and Salim died, she hardly thought of him at all. She certainly didn't miss him. He'd been, for the past year if not more, the means to an end, that end being the land. And now that she'd achieved it, he was of no importance. She wasn't proud of feeling that way, in fact, she was a bit ashamed, but not ashamed enough to dim her pride in acquisition. She'd heard about Dris' death, and that too seemed to her like a story from another time and place. She reminded herself with a start that it was very likely Dris' death was related to Salim's, and it surprised her that other people still cared about Salim and anything he'd done. She was a terrible wife, she told herself, and cold. But it really didn't bother her, which just proved how very cold she was.

Another widow in the kampong was also wondering how she'd gotten so cold. Latifah would never say so publicly, but she too did not miss her late husband, even though they'd been married many years and she'd been a good wife to him in her own estimation, given what she'd had to work with. She'd never berated him for his lack of interest in her, encouraging him instead to be a caring father. Nor had she ever tasked him with his feelings toward Nik Man, though she could see what they were, and at the beginning, it had wounded her deeply. She got used to it, though, and all those years, Dris had his food cooked, his laundry done and his sexual orientation unquestioned. Latifah couldn't see how she could have done more, and she considered any obligation to him discharged.

Talk about Dris had now reached a crescendo, and she believed that in the coming weeks it would begin to die down. It could never be maintained at this frantic level, and soon enough not only would the talk have faded, but there would be nothing that would ever bring it to life again. She'd feared this talk for years, though nothing ever came of it, and that fear was lifting. People would say everything they had to say about him now, and then they'd get bored with him as a topic of conversation, and her life would actually improve.

Maybe she'd marry again. Or maybe not – there was a lot to be said for having no one tell you what to do, or expect anything from you. She'd see what was in store, but believed things were definitely looking up.

Chapter XXVI

Osman decided the time was ripe for an in-depth interview of Omar, who'd been cooling his heels for several days, being served his meals by Zul, who, following the lead of his hero Rahman, was rigidly correct with Omar but no warmer than that. Rahman would not easily forgive either Omar, or his lackey Hatim, for scaring his mother-in-law half to death, and frightening his wife-to-be just hearing about it. He must recognize, Rahman thought, that this was Rahman's family, and not available for people to think they could try to intimidate them.

Omar was brought into the meeting room, where Zul laid out curry puffs (an office favourite) coffee and cigarettes, and fixed Omar with a baleful stare when he sat down. Osman had sent a car for Maryam and Rubiah, but began the questioning before they arrived.

'Why, Che Omar?'

'Why what, Police Chief Osman?'

'Don't start like that,' Osman advised him. 'I'm already unhappy with you, and if you want to pretend you don't know what we're talking about, we can save some time and you can sit in your cell for a while more and think about it.'

Osman had never been this stern, and this fed up with suspects. He wondered whether he was being hardened by the job, or maybe growing into it.

'I didn't really do anything,' Omar began.

'Really do anything?' Osman pounced. 'What does that mean?'

Omar sighed and began again. 'No, it's just. Well, I think we've started badly. Let me begin again. I didn't kill anyone. Not Salim. Not anyone. My biggest mistake was dealing with Salim and not staying loyal to Nik Man, who was my client, and whom I should have supported. I admit that, and I'm sorry for it.'

Osman nodded. 'Why, Che Omar?' he repeated.

Omar hung his head, and Osman dismissed it as grandstanding. 'I was greedy. I thought I could make a little more money and no one would ever know about it. I never thought Salim would win! That was a surprise.

'And then, I underestimated what a loudmouth Salim really was. That he would tell Nik Man! I never thought that would happen.'

'From what everyone's told me about him, including his wife, this was well known. Everyone I've spoken to has said what an overbearing fool he was. And you, as a bomoh, you should be able to read people better than most. Why then would you depend on Salim's discretion. Salim of all people!'

'I can't disagree, now that it's happened. You're right, of course, I know that. But you know, Salim always tried one thing and another and then moved on. I thought this kite-flying thing would be the same. And I thought he'd lose, so why brag about anything. Why poke a stick at Nik Man? I don't know. Maybe I should have known …'

Maryam and Rubiah knocked at the door and walked in, followed by Zul making obeisance, hurrying to provide coffee and asking for any special requests. Rahman smiled and remained in his corner, taking notes.

'I'm just asking, Mak Cik, about why Che Omar here thought he'd provide jampi for Salim and no one would every know.'

'It does seem a major … miscalculation,' Maryam agreed.

'I know that now,' Omar replied with a bit of spirit. 'Now of course, I see what a terrible mistake I made.'

'I believe that mistake might have started this whole affair,' Maryam told him.

'Maybe,' he said, looking uncomfortable. 'It wasn't a good decision.'

Rubiah snorted. 'No, as decisions go, it wasn't.'

'You've said,' Osman informed him, 'that this was all a question of greed.'

'Yes,' Omar nodded, solidly behind the story.

'How much did you charge Salim for the jampi?'

'What?'

'Well, a question of greed, the money would be of paramount importance, wouldn't it? So you must have the sum in your mind.'

Omar looked confused. 'Well, it wasn't just these jampi, it was also for the future.'

'What future?' Osman was relentless. 'You said just a moment ago that you thought this would just be a way to make a little money, that you thought Salim would lose, and therefore he wouldn't tell anyone because no one would care. Am I right, Man?'

Rahman looked at his notes and nodded solemnly. 'Exactly.'

'Well, you know, maybe not a future with Salim.'

'With who then?'

'Just to get a few ringgit, that's all.'

'OK. How many ringgit?'

Omar hung his head. 'He paid me 50 ringgit.'

Everyone stared at him.

'You started all this, and risked your relationship with Nik Man for 50 ringgit? That's your excuse?'

'I wasn't, it was just … you know, some money,' Omar bleated.

'You took such a risk for that? I can't believe it,' Maryam announced.

No one seemed to believe it. 'So let me clarify,' Osman summed up. 'You risked a relationship you've had for a long time, with a man who paid you more than that every month, and who won tournaments reliably, to make 50 ringgit with someone likely to insult people and tell your secret? Am I understanding this correctly?'

'When you say it like that, it sounds crazy.'

'How would you like me to say it? Go ahead. Try.'

Omar struggled for a moment before he started to speak. 'It was just to make money. I know it sounds crazy, like I said, but I just wanted to make some extra money. It would be a problem if I got caught, but I really thought no one would ever know.'

'And then what happened?'

'What?'

'When Salim told Nik Man.'

'Oh Nik Man was furious. He was already pretty irritated because his kite was cut and Salim was telling everyone how well he'd done and how he'd beaten the champions. No one likes to hear that kind of talk: you don't usually hear it at a tournament. The winner may brag to his friends or family at home, but not at the tournament in front of everyone who played. But Salim had no manners.

'Anyway, as you can imagine, Nik Man was already feeling the loss of his kite, and then Salim bragging, and then Salim told him that his jampi came from me. Nik Man turned and looked at me, and I was frightened. I'd never gotten such a look from him, or from anyone else. Why Salim had to say something I'll never know, but it was out.'

'I understand you rarely came to tournaments.'

'That's true. I don't go much. I do the jampi, that's enough for me. I don't have to see it.'

'Why were you there on that day?'

'Because of Salim.' He hung his head, but Osman couldn't tell if it was contrition or just dramatics. 'I thought I'd see what he did. I was also, if I'm honest, a little nervous about what Salim might say. As it happens, I was right.'

'Wouldn't it have been better if you weren't there, in that case? Nik Man might have cooled off a little before he spoke to you.'

'I don't know why I went. I just felt I should be there.'

'Did you think about killing Salim beforehand?'

'What? I didn't think about killing Salim at all,' he said indignantly. 'Not before, not after. I wasn't there to kill anyone.'

'It seems to me,' Maryam broke in for the first time, having sat silent up to this point, 'It makes more sense to think of you going to the contest to kill Salim than going for reasons you can't really explain, and don't make sense. Nik Man is your primary client, but you never go to his contests. And here is a man you say you never liked and didn't trust, and you made 50 ringgit on the jampi, but you travel here to spend a couple of hours watching him fly. I don't understand that.'

Omar stammered a little and said nothing.

'I think Salim told you he was going to tell Nik Man, or you suspected it, and you went to shut him up, however that had to be done.' Maryam leaned back in her seat and regarded Omar. 'But you were too late. What I just don't get, Che Omar, is why you had anything to do with Salim at all? I don't understand. Explain it to me.'

He stared at Maryam as though he'd never seen her before, and suddenly lurched forward to take a long sip of his coffee.

'I wanted to see if my jampi worked.' Now it was Maryam's turn to goggle at Omar. 'You know, a little experiment which went horribly wrong. I gave Salim a special jampi. I didn't tell him about it, because what would be the point of that? He didn't know anything about jampi, or kites either for that matter. So you see it was a good way of finding out if this jampi could make even someone who knew nothing and had no talent become a winner.'

'Scientific,' Maryam commented.

'Like that,' Omar nodded. 'And it worked. It was my jampi

that won, not Salim. Salim was *macam itik mendengarkan guntur*: like a duck listening to thunder. He understood absolutely nothing about what he was doing. So how could he win?' A rhetorical flourish. 'He didn't. It was my jampi. And I was going to tell Nik Man about it, after the contest, and then give him the jampi, but then Salim told him first and Nik Man didn't want to listen to my explanation.'

'I'm not surprised,' Osman said drily. 'It isn't the most convincing.'

'Maybe not, but it's true.' Osman grimaced. If it were true, it certainly didn't sound it. However …

'I was trying to tell this to Nik Man, but he wouldn't listen. He told me he'd never work with me again. Not very fair, after all the years we'd been together.'

'He could say the same about you,' Osman pointed out.

'Yes, but there was a *reason*,' Omar insisted. 'I just told you. An experiment.'

Could it just be ridiculous enough to be true, Osman wondered? Or a badly thought out excuse. 'And what about Hatim? What kind of an experiment was that?'

Chapter XXVII

In fact, the case was not solved before the wedding, as Ashikin had ordered, but it was essentially forgotten by all those caught up in the festivities. Aliza looked beautiful, as everyone thought she would, and Rahman supremely happy. His mother, who had nursed him through his injuries when his life had been despaired of, had tears in her eyes and she saw her son happy and healthy and married. There were times when she thought this day would never come, and here it was. His father beamed next to her, nodding and smiling as he watched his son sit in state next to Aliza, looking handsome and strong.

Aliza and Rahman sat on their 'thrones' and accepted the good wishes of all their guests, while four little girls stood behind them with ceremonial fans. Rubiah's daughter Teh was in charge of the girls, standing next to them and urging them to pay attention to their duties, which they did intermittently. Aliza could hear the whispers and occasional threats if she tried to listen, but decided instead to block it out and concentrate on the guests before her.

Tables and chairs were draped with white songket, the best quality of course. Ashikin and Rosnah, assisted by an army of younger cousins, had beautifully decorated the room. It was just what Aliza wanted, though Aliza herself hadn't realized it. It was only when she saw the room this morning, with it's fabric flowers and decorated eggs and swags of songket everywhere that she drew in her breath in delight, and saw that when she pictured her wedding, indeed, this is what she'd imagined. She wasn't sure how Ashikin had so unerringly known this, since Aliza gave her almost no instruction, but that was Ashikin, somehow knowing what people were thinking before they knew it themselves.

Maryam and Mamat marvelled at their good fortune: the marriage, the grandchildren, a son-in-law with a wonderful career and a daughter about to become a teacher. It was better than Mamat had ever imagined, and he smiled throughout the whole ceremony.

'What a couple!' Rubiah enthused. 'They're so perfect for each other. So happy. I'm so proud!' She too smiled beneficently upon the new couple, who, instead of sitting immobile in their seats were actually whispering to each other and laughing softly. Ashikin went up to Aliza ostensibly to straighten her hair, and then hissed at her to look dignified. Aliza giggled at her too, and Ashikin gave up. She could hardly pinch the bride's ear or lecture her, so she resigned herself to letting Aliza do what she wanted. She sat down again with Rosnah, and the two compared notes on their pregnancies.

Maryam watched Yi, growing taller each day, lurch dangerously toward a tray of cakes, and she shut her eyes in case he fell into them – she didn't want to witness it. When she opened them, Yi was already sitting with his cousins offering a napkin full of cakes around to everyone. She prayed he'd fill out soon, or at least learn to control his feet, but clearly that prayer was not to be granted this afternoon. She too went up to Aliza, not even bothering to pretend to fix her hair, and whispered to her how beautiful everything was, and her hopes for their happiness throughout their marriage. Rahman leaned over and thanked her, and then Maryam backed out of the way so the photographers could take innumerable pictures, at least one of which was guaranteed to hang in their living room for the rest of their lives.

The entire Kota Bharu police department was there, trying to make Rahman laugh and otherwise smoking cigarettes and laughing at one another. In another country, these men would have taken over the bar, but liquor was forbidden to Muslims and soft drinks were the order of the day. Still, the police contingent managed to be as rowdy sober as many others might have needed to be drunk to achieve, and so burnished their reputations.

Aliza could not believe it when the wedding ended. So much work and planning, which obsessed her whole family for months, and now it was over. It was hard to imagine her life without a wedding looming in the near future, obscuring anything that came after it. And here she was, on the other side, a place to which she never thought she'd actually arrive. She looked shyly at Rahman, in this, the first moments of their life together, and suddenly was nervous, as Aliza almost never was. They went back to a small house Rahman had rented for them in Kampong Penambang, close to Maryam, Rubiah and Ashikin. Both sets of parents had made sure the house was furnished and ready for them, and Aliza stepped in to the first place in her life she would live without her family. It was daunting, but Rahman seemed to be a bit overwhelmed himself, so she didn't feel alone.

'They did a nice job', Rahman said uncertainly, looking around at the house, which was now his. 'It looks great.'

Aliza nodded and tried to look perky rather than anxious. She tried to shade that unfamiliar feeling, and didn't want to ruin the moment being tongue-tied and stiff. She'd read her share of romances, and been instructed by Ashikin and her mother (Ashikin's instruction was much more helpful and straightforward) about her wedding night, and it seemed to her, although no one had said so in so many words, that things would go better if she was upbeat and affectionate. Nervousness in either of them might simply spoil the mood, whatever that was supposed to be. Aliza had been very clear on the mood concept when discussing it before, but now that she was in it, it was more amorphous. Still, nothing would go wrong because she wasn't trying her best, so she smiled as broadly as she could and told Rahman how happy she was to be married to him. He returned the complement with fervour, and both of them stood awkwardly in the living room, not looking at the bedroom, until Aliza announced she'd have to change out of her songket. Rahman immediately offered to help, and things began to move fairly smoothly after that.

* * *

Some days after the wedding, Osman was back at work, talking to Omar, who insisted he did not kill Salim, did not know who did, and refused to discuss the luckless Hatim, who was still sitting in his cell.

Hatim had already told all he knew, which was precious little: Omar knew him casually, and had approached him to do a job, which he assured him would be easy, painless and for which he would get paid. Hatim, a widower with little money, jumped at the chance. He freely admitted to Osman that once it was explained to him it seemed kind of odd. He was to find the largest black spiders he could, and bring them to a stall in the market. He was to go at night and place them inside the stall, and then turn up the next morning to monitor the mayhem, which would invariably follow the discovery.

He dutifully collected the spiders, though he wasn't happy about it, and saved them in a box. He assured Osman he considered getting food for them, but could not really catch flies and other insects, and birds were out of the question. Osman was feeling a little queasy hearing about it and was glad to know there would be no detailed description of their dinner.

He went at night to get into the stall, but was unable to break the lock or the boards guarding it. Unsure of what to do, he carved notches in the shelf, which he thought looked ominous, and might frighten the woman who owned it because they were inexplicable. Osman cursed himself for trying to figure out those notches when he now knew they were randomly made by an idiot. A waste of time, he told himself, but unfortunately it was not the first time and neither would it be the last.

He climbed up, looking for an opening between the roof and

the sideboards, and found a small chink in the wood, through which he pushed one of the spiders, who promptly died. He left the body there: firstly, he couldn't reach it, secondly, he was tired and finally, he thought it looked scary. And it did, he confirmed: that woman was scared. He kept the second one and resolved to go back the next day to see what was happening.

Imagine his surprise, he told Osman, to find nothing at all happening! Things were as usual, and the woman in the stall didn't look frightened at all. He deduced from this she hadn't seen the spider, and that the notches had not been eerie enough. Oh! And for atmosphere, he rubbed some chicken blood, into which a feather or two might have ended up, under the shelf, and stuck a picture of a spider there because he couldn't put a live one right there or it would fall down. Osman wondered if Hatim had been this slow all his life, or was it just now, so that it could annoy him. All these 'clues', which he had actually spent time thinking about, were the work of a mindless fool. And Mamat had even wasted time cleaning off the damned chicken blood.

Anyway, Hatim continued, he then reached in for his second spider, which had unfortunately been crushed on the way over because the box it was in fell in the back of the pedicab seat. He took the dead spider and tried to place it under the fabric without the woman noticing him, but she watched him, so he had no choice but to pull it out in his hand and scare her with it. It actually worked, all hell broke loose, culminating in her vomiting on him and the rest Osman already knew.

Osman thanked him for his story and sent him back to his cell, then sat in his office, behind his desk, with his head in his hands. It was unbelievable, all these clues which meant absolutely nothing, just a comedy of errors. After a minute or two he picked up his head and started to laugh, and felt like he'd never stop.

Chapter XXVIII

'All right, Che Omar,' Osman told him, still laughing to himself. 'I've spoken to your employee, Che Hatim, and he's told me the whole sorry story. You hired him, why, I can't tell you, since he doesn't seem as if he could walk a straight line. However, that's not my business. So, you hired him to scare Mak Cik Maryam, presumably to get her to drop the case, right?'

Omar looked a bit stunned and a bit sour faced, and Osman could sympathize with both those states. 'Come on, tell me,' Osman said. 'I already know. And I'm getting very tired of you thinking you're so clever.' Osman lit a cigarette and did not offer one to Omar, though it bothered him not to, and to be rude. 'Because anyone who was at all clever wouldn't go near Hatim, especially for something which requires thought. I don't know what you were thinking, but I suppose it makes things easier for me.'

Omar leaned back in his seat, thinking.

'The truth now,' Osman warned him. 'I'm all out of patience.'

'I had to. I promised Sharifah.'

'Sharifah?' This was a surprise.

Omar nodded, looking semi-miserable. Mixed in with that

was pure irritation.

'Why?'

He swallowed hard. 'She was afraid of an investigation. Not that she had anything to fear,' he was quick to add. 'But she was tired of Mak Cik Maryam coming over and asking so many questions.'

'Innocent people don't usually ask favours like that.'

'Sometimes they do,' answered Omar, who apparently knew a good deal about police investigations. Osman could easily envision himself in an argument along the lines of 'No they don't', 'Yes they do' and decided to say nothing.

'When did she ask you to do this?'

'A week ago, maybe. Something like that.'

'This was all before Dris died.'

Omar nodded.

Osman leaned in to him. 'Was it Sharifah who asked you, or Nik Man?'

'Sharifah.'

'Did Nik Man know?'

Suddenly there was a new emotion appearing in his eyes, edging out annoyance and misery. It was fear.

'I don't know,' he mumbled.

'Did Nik Man kill Salim?'

'No.'

'Did you?'

'No. I don't know who did it.'

Osman was now completely convinced that was a lie, but he was also sure Omar wouldn't tell him now. Whoever killed Salim,

Omar was more afraid of them than he was of Osman, which was a bit insulting, but Osman had never cultivated a tough police persona so maybe it made sense.

Osman let Omar sit in silence before him as he ticked through the case in his mind. Who was left as a suspect? Dris was dead, so if he had killed Salim, no one need fear him anymore. Nik Man and Sharifah. Bahiyah. That would make sense: he could see how someone would fear Bahiyah. And then the widows, who looked peaceable enough, but perhaps underneath that were really frightening.

He circled back to Sharifah. She was so pretty, Osman thought, he hated to think of her killing Salim, and to the best of his knowledge Sharifah wasn't even at the contest. But there was something about her that spooked Maryam, who did not scare easily, and led Maryam to put the papaya aside for fear of poisoning. He wanted to ask her what it was about Sharifah, and stood up to go to the market to find her. Omar went back to his cell to contemplate what he wanted to tell the police, and Osman went to the main market.

* * *

Maryam was at her stall, just as he'd hoped, though it was the time of the afternoon when things began to slow down. She was relaxing with an iced coffee and a cigarette, ready, however, to abandon them at a moment's notice should a customer appear.

Osman walked up and smiled, and she greeted him good-naturedly. 'You have a question,' she stated.

'I do. But it isn't a yes or no answer.'

She nodded and waited for him to begin.

'Why were you so nervous about Sharifah, and wouldn't eat the papaya? What was it the made you think she'd poison you?'

'Well, I was wrong,' Maryam pointed out. 'She wasn't trying to poison me, so are you sure you still want me to talk about it?' Osman nodded. 'First, she came to visit at dinnertime. She told me it was because she couldn't find anyone to look after her kids until them, and perhaps that was true. But at the time I thought it was very strange. No one goes visiting at that time.

'And she came all the way to Kampong Penambang to say she was sorry, which seemed ... excessive. However, in light of the fact I was wrong about her, perhaps I was suspicious of her for no reason, and she was just telling the truth.

'There's something about her though. She's very pretty,' she gave him a sharp look and he blushed, 'and talks very nicely, but there's steel in there. She's a prettier, quieter, smarter version of Bahiyah. Bahiyah advertises how tough she is, Sharifah advertises how nice she is, but she's just like her older sister.'

'I hadn't really thought of Sharifah and Bahiyah together,' Osman admitted. 'And I should have. It would have made me look at Sharifah differently.'

'They are sisters.'

'I should go and see Nik Man again.'

Maryam made no comment.

'I may have overlooked things.'

'Do you want me to go with you?' Maryam asked.

Osman nodded. 'I'll help you close up if you want to go now.

And by the way,' he added, cheering up now that she was going with him, 'I spoke to Hatim today to get his story on what he did to you. You won't believe it.'

Chapter XXIX

They arrived in Kampong Banggol at the end of the afternoon, though not as late as Sharifah had come to Maryam's house. Still, the shadows were long and Maryam was a bit uncomfortable about intruding. 'Maybe we should wait until tomorrow, when we can come earlier,' she whispered to Osman.

He shook his head. 'Now's a good time.'

It did not seem the best time for Sharifah and Nik Man, who were trying to get their two boys cleaned up while dinner was simmering. They were nonplussed to see the police at their door, and stared for a brief moment before their manners took over and they did the right thing.

'Come in, come in,' Nik Man invited them, gesturing to the living room couch. He was still holding a wriggling little boy in his arms, who was being put into a T-shirt but fighting it. 'One second,' he promised and hoisted the boy on his shoulder and brought him into the bedroom. He emerged two minutes later with a boy in a T-shirt hanging on to his arm. Sharifah was still struggling with her son, and Nik Man admonished him sternly. 'We have guests,' he told him. Now let Mak and Ayah talk to them and you two go and play inside. And put on your shirt,' he added as the two scampered away.

Nik Man turned his attention to Maryam and Osman. 'Sit, sit, we'll have some coffee in a moment.'

'No, no really, we'll be going home to dinner any minute and we don't want to put you to any trouble.'

Sharifah and Nik Man exchanged a look, which said if they didn't want to put them to any trouble they wouldn't be here, but as Sharifah had already officially apologized for just such an attitude, she rearranged her expression into polite interest and watched them carefully.

Osman ploughed right into his opening remarks. 'Omar told me today that he'd hired someone to go to Mak Cik Maryam's stall and frighten her. Of course, I told him he'd picked the wrong person, because Mak Cik Maryam is one of the bravest people I know.' Maryam tried to look modest rather than amazed.

'His plan didn't go very well, you may already know, and the perpetrator was arrested.'

'And I believe thrown up on,' Nik Man added, grinning.

'That too,' Osman agreed. However, no matter how amusing the episode was, and it did have its moments, at heart it was a cruel, heartless and dangerous act that might well have led to serious harm. We're very lucky it turned out to be a farce rather than a tragedy.' Sharifah looked slightly baffled by the analogy though Maryam was sure she understood the gist.

'And Omar told me he planned it because you had asked him, Cik Sharifah. And that you had told him what you wanted done.'

The room was dead silent. Sharifah's face was still, she didn't even blink. Nik Man looked bewildered.

'Sharifah?' he asked. 'No, you have it wrong. It can't be.'

'It can be, and I was told it's true. But what I want to know is why?'

'How can you ask her why she did something she didn't do? It doesn't make sense to me. Sharifah? Are you going to say anything?'

She sat silent, examining her hands, wishing herself elsewhere. She had worked so hard to make sure her family and her world stayed safe and all that effort now seemed to be for nothing.

'You know, Omar is quite undependable. I have experience with him, and I will never use him again.' Nik Man was adamant. 'I wouldn't believe anything he tells you.'

'You may well be right,' Osman agreed. 'He can be very tricky, and certainly disloyal. But is he lying about this? Even a liar may sometimes tell the truth.'

'Not this one,' Nik Man insisted. 'I regret ever knowing him.'

'I'm sure,' Maryam said. 'After what he did to you. But Cik Sharifah, we haven't heard from you yet.'

Sharifah looked up as if she had just woken from sleep. 'From me?' she asked vaguely.

Maryam was becoming impatient. 'Cik Sharifah, please. We all have things to do.'

'Don't bully her,' Nik Man ordered.

'Let's not get angry,' Osman refereed. 'These are important questions.'

Sharifah sighed, and brushed the hair back from her face. She was really very pretty, Maryam had to admit. 'I ... may have ... said, well, something, but I didn't ... mean for him to do anything, and if he frightened you in any way, Mak Cik, I take responsibility for it.'

'Very nice, Cik Sharifah, but what did you do and why?'

'I, it's hard to explain.'

'Try.'

She became slightly tearful, and it looked quite charming, but Maryam wasn't having any. 'Yes?'

'I was ... afraid of you.'

'Of me?'

'Of the police, of you, of the whole situation. You're accustomed to this, Mak Cik, you do it all the time. For other people, simple kampong people like we are, it's frightening. We don't know about all these things: our world is small.' She opened her eyes wider. *Katak dibawah tempurong:* frogs under a coconut shell, that's what we are. I didn't know what would happen to us, to our children. I just wanted it all to stop.

'But I was wrong.' She gave a delicate sniff. 'I know that. I even knew it when I spoke to him but I was ... I let my fear get the better of me and I acted on that fear.'

'And what did you ask him to do, exactly.'

'It's hard for me to remember.'

'Once again, Cik Sharifah, try.'

'Well, I asked him to discourage you from investigating any more, just to stop.' She looked at Maryam earnestly. 'Not to hurt you in any way, but to make you decide to drop it.'

'And did you tell him how to do it?'

Sharifah shook her head. 'No, I really couldn't think of anything. But Che Omar, he's a bomoh, he knows what to do even when we don't.'

'Omar,' Nik Mat spit. 'If I see him again …'

'Don't even think that,' Maryam ordered. 'Don't go in that direction.' Nik Man subsided. 'So, to be clear,' Maryam said, watching Osman, 'you asked Che Omar, the bomoh your husband is never going to speak to again, to frighten me off the case because I, and Police Chief Osman here, scared you and you wanted it to stop. As to how to frighten me, you left it entirely up to Che Omar to decide. Now however, you believe it is wrong and you're sorry, but you were overcome by fear and intimidation and acted on impulse. Am I correct?'

Osman could see Maryam was seething under her veneer of courtesy, and he really didn't hold it against her.

'Yes, you've put it together very well, Mak Cik, although when you say it so clearly in such an organized way it sounds a little silly of me.'

Silly? Maryam wanted to rage at her. You call threatening a respectable mak cik who has done nothing to you with spiders, silly? You can kill someone like that. But she said nothing about it.

Osman watched Sharifah carefully: 'I know you have just said you were frightened by the investigation,' – Sharifah nodded – 'but I think there's something more.' Nik Man, sitting next to her, bristled. 'I think you were protecting someone.' Sharifah paled.

'Oh, you may have been frightened, but that wouldn't make you act as you did. Did you think your husband killed Salim?' Sharifah stared at him as she would at a snake. 'Did you think we wouldn't ever look past what you told us?'

'Did you kill him?' he asked Nik Man.

'No,' he croaked, but he didn't look convinced.

Osman rose from his seat. 'I think you'd both better come to the station. Is there family you can call to watch the children?'

With a trembling lower lip, Sharifah went for Bahiyah, and Nik Man sat silent, smoking, listening to his boys play in the bedroom. Sharifah returned with Bahiyah ready for battle, and she snapped at Osman even before she walked into the room.

'What is this I hear? Taking them to the station? I can't believe I'm hearing this! And leaving their children? What's the matter with you?' She addressed the last to Maryam. Before she could answer, Osman stepped in.

'This is a police matter, Mak Cik. I know it's upsetting, but this is the law. Are we ready?'

Maryam was proud of Osman. When she'd first met him, years ago, that speech would have reduced him nearly to tears, and Maryam would have had to answer for him. But he had matured in his job, and could now stand up for himself. Maryam felt much of the credit for this was due to her tutelage.

They trooped out of the house and into the car, with Bahiyah staring after them like Medusa.

Chapter XXX

They were separated at the station. Maryam sat with Sharifah – Osman deemed his policemen too likely to fall under her sway if left to guard her. The car was sent to pick up Rubiah and Aliza so they too could add their opinion to what was transpiring.

Nik Man looked nervous, more than nervous: scared. He tried to keep himself still, but kept breaking out in finger tapping and foot swinging. Rahman gave him cigarettes and the ever-popular curry puffs, but he wasn't interested in food. He was gulping coffee, though, and Rahman feared if he stoked his unease with caffeine he might explode altogether. Rahman pitied him, and for reasons he could not articulate felt Nik Man was innocent, but inarticulate reasons are none at all, so he waited to see if something more concrete occurred to him.

Osman walked in, and sat down quietly across the table. 'Nik Man,' he said in a soft and friendly voice, 'is there anything else we can get you? A cold drink, perhaps?'

Nik Man shook his head and looked down at his lap.

'Nik Man, please tell me what happened at the contest.'

'I've already told you.'

'Tell me again.'

'I'm not sure I understand,' Rahman interjected, hoping to be a comforting force for Nik Man. 'Please, I would like to prove your innocence.'

Nik Man stared at him, as though he couldn't process what he'd heard. Osman was surprised as well, not expecting that approach, but it wasn't a bad one.

'I was at the contest. I lost. Salim won ...'

'Wait, back up,' Rahman ordered. 'Start from the beginning. Did you go alone?'

'No, of course not. I went with Dris.' He looked bereft for a moment. 'I always went with Dris. He had all the stuff we might need.'

'Such as?'

'Extra string, some glass, glue, I don't know what else. Water, I guess. You can get thirsty flying in the sun.'

Rahman nodded. 'Go on.'

'So, Dris and I got there. I got my kite ready. I go over it, make sure it's in good condition, no tears or anything, the string is tight. Everything was fine. Dris and I were waiting for it to start.'

'Was Salim there? Did you talk to him?'

'He was there but I didn't talk to him.'

'Did you see Omar there?'

Nik Man shook his head.

'Did you see Halimah, Salim's wife?'

'I didn't see her either. Of course, I wasn't looking for her, or anyone else, as I was paying attention to the kite and getting myself ready.'

Rahman nodded encouragingly.

'Then the contest started, and my kite went up.' Nik Man lost his nervousness and began to talk more fluently as he talked about kites. 'It was flying pretty well, doing a lot of loops and fancy stuff, because you have to, in a contest. But I thought it was going well. Some fighting with other kites but it was still a bit early so nothing really serious.

'I saw Salim's kite, a real beauty. It was way too good a kite for a flyer like him. He was kind of awkward with it – the kite was flying him, if you know what I mean. Anyway, he kept his kite in the thick of it, but no fancy moves; he was having enough trouble just keeping it aloft. It's harder than it looks. It almost got away from him a few times but he managed to hold on to it.

'Then he moves his kite over near mine, as though he wanted to fight with me, and before I knew it, he'd jerked his kite string and cut mine, and my kite went off into the sky. I knew it wasn't coming back, I could see that. And by the way he moved it, I also knew it was a mistake. He had no idea what he was doing. He cut my kite by accident, can you believe it? I've lost before, many times, but never by accident. It's so infuriating.

'And Salim starts laughing and shouting that he beat me. The other flyers, they ignored him. No one liked him, we all know how we're supposed to act. If you win this time you may lose the next so there's no point in being too proud, you know. But he was yelling and laughing. I tried to ignore it. No point in getting angry. I went back to sit with Dris and talk about it. We were both shocked. But he won the tournament.

'Everyone was surprised by it. No one was happy. But again, it's a contest and you have to take it well no matter what happens.

But he was dancing around, congratulating himself, because no one else would. Well, beginner's luck. It happens. And then I saw Omar. Omar never comes to these things. Never. All the years he's done my jampi for me, he's never come to see me fly. So I walk up to him, but Salim is now jumping around in front of him screaming, "I won, I won!" And it suddenly hit me: Omar must have given jampi to Salim also.

'Another huge shock for me. He betrayed me. I was speechless, I tell you. I couldn't think of a thing to say except stare at Omar. Then Salim turned around and said something like you didn't know? Yes, I got my jampi from Omar, and I won. What about you? Omar is looking kind of embarrassed, as he should be. He started to stammer some story about trying out something new but I didn't want to listen. Once someone betrays you like that you can't go back. I knew right there I'd never speak to Omar again, and I'd find another bomoh to help me. I was done.

'I began shouting at Omar, I admit it. If Omar had been killed then, it would have been me. But he's still alive, so I didn't actually do anything. I was afraid I'd hit him if I stayed there, so I left.'

'Left the tournament?'

'No, you saw me there when you arrived, didn't you? I left Omar and Salim. I couldn't stand it anymore.'

'Neither could Dris, could he? I mean, Salim had just told so many people about him loving you.'

Nik Man sighed. 'Isn't it odd to say loving you as though it was the worst thing anyone could accuse him of? I'm not saying there was anything to it, or that anything ... happened. Nothing did. Nothing.'

'I understand,' Rahman assured him. 'But it would seem to me that both you and Dris would be angry at Salim beyond what happened with Omar.'

'Yes,' he nodded absently. 'Of course we were.'

'Is there something wrong, Nik Man?' Rahman asked. He suddenly looked deflated, if that was the correct word, beaten. Rahman did not think it was because he was mourning Salim.

'No, nothing. You were asking?'

'You walked away from Salim and Omar.'

'Yes, I couldn't stand being around them anymore. Both of them were useless, faithless even. No loyalty in either of them. Not ...'

'Not?'

Nik Man began to weep. He cried like a man cries, as though his sobs were torn out of him against his will. He bent over in the chair and covered his face. It was real grief, deep grief, and Rahman wasn't sure what to do. Osman came out from behind his desk with tissues and an alarmed look on his face. He looked at Rahman, who shrugged, but then bent over Nik Man as he would over a younger brother and stroked his back.

'Don't cry. It won't change anything. Everything will be fine, you'll see. You'll be happy again, I know it.' Nik Man ignored him at first and then raised a tear-stained face to him. 'It won't,' he coughed. 'It will never be fine again. Dris is gone, you see, and he was my best friend.'

Rahman didn't know what to say to this. The only thing that came to mind were religious platitudes, and they seemed not quite what was necessary. Instead, he stood next to Nik Man silently, his hand on his back, hoping that his just being there would be of some comfort to him.

When Nik Man cried himself out, he looked up and silently accepted the tissues. After than, Rahman signalled for more coffee, and offered him a cigarette to calm his nerves. Osman remained sitting on his desk in front of Nik Man, and Rahman sat right beside him. To an uninformed observer, the grouping would look more like a gathering of close friends than an interrogation.

'Is it Dris?' Osman asked softly, when they are all in control again.

Nik Man nodded, but kept his eyes locked on the window behind Osman.

'You miss him,' Rahman said sympathetically.

'Of course. We were always together, ever since we were kids. *Macam kuku dengan isinya:* like the nail and the quick. I always loved kites and Dris was always with me. I can't imagine how I'm going to fly now without Dris.' He sniffed.

'Maybe you can start teaching your son, Nik Man. It will give you time together.'

Nik Man nodded. 'It's a good idea.'

'What do you think happened to Dris?'

'I know what happened. I killed him.'

Chapter XXXI

They stared at him.

'I know, I can't believe it myself. But they wouldn't leave me alone, all day and all night.'

'Who?'

'Sharifah and Bahiyah. They told me we'd be ruined when everyone started gossiping about Salim's tales. That our kids would be teased and worse at school. We'd be forced to move, I don't know what else. Do you think that's true?' he asked pathetically.

It was a bit late for that conversation, Rahman thought, and wasn't sure what to say. Of course, in the end gossip would die down, especially if Dris stayed with his wife and both he and Nik Man went about their business and denied it. People were not looking to condemn them, even if this salacious gossip would be too good not to repeat. But what good was it to tell him that now? And to say that Sharifah and her sister were right? That seemed wrong as well. So Rahman made non-committal noises and hoped it passed for an answer. Nik Man didn't seem to be listening anyway.

'And then?' Osman prompted.

'Then, they kept on me all the time. Salim was dead, and by the way, I didn't kill him, though I wish I killed him instead of Dris. I wouldn't be sad about it at all. They said Dris was weak, and that if people asked him about it he'd end up telling them and then our family would be ruined.'

'Ruined' sounded pretty melodramatic, Rahman knew. After all, all of them here were from peasant families; they weren't royalty who could be deposed. How could they be ruined when no one had actually done anything? Rahman stuck to his belief that it would have blown over, given time, and people would move on to gossiping about something else. That wouldn't help Nik Man, however.

'Bahiyah told me that Sharifah would have to leave with the kids if I didn't do anything. That Sharifah could not risk destroying our children's lives for Dris. I don't know,' he moaned softly, 'I didn't think it was so terrible. But I didn't want Sharifah to leave. I love her,' he said plaintively.

Rahman nodded encouragingly.

'I talked to Sharifah,' Nik Man continued. 'I asked her if she'd really leave me. I don't think she wanted to, but she was so used to listening to her sister, it was hard for her to go against her. If Bahiyah thought it was important, eventually Sharifah would too.' He hung his head.

'And they told you, they advised you to kill Nik Man?' Rahman could tell by Osman's tone he was still trying to understand this.

'They said I had to.' They both regarded Nik Man, a person they'd thought of as calm and strong and rational, an excellent husband and devoted father, a good friend and a customer who would not countenance disloyalty. And here he was in front of them, reduced to tears and regret, which they both believed would haunt him for the rest of his life.

'I ignored them at first. I had no intention of ever killing Dris. He was my friend! I didn't want to kill him. But they told me the choice was between my family and Dris, between Sharifah staying and Dris. I think I should have called her bluff, and see if she would have left me. She probably would have: Bahiyah would have gone to work on her and it would have been over. But even so, I wouldn't feel like this. I'll never get over this. Dris will be with me until I die, asking me why I would do this to someone so loyal to me. And do I have an answer? No.

'I have no excuse and no answer. I'm as guilty as can be. You should hang me.' Rahman and Osman both made comforting noises. 'I deserve it. I deserve to meet Dris and beg his forgiveness. And I wouldn't blame him,' he began crying again, 'if he refused. How could I have been so wrong?'

Osman didn't know what to say. There was no right answer.

'Even though I did it to save Sharifah, now I don't care anymore,' he said miserably. When I look at her I see Dris. In the end I would have lost both, once I killed Dris. I should have just told her to leave. *Bertukar jiwa dengan semangat:* I exchanged my life force for my soul. Now he's gone and I don't know what to do.'

'How did you kill him?' It seemed such a cold question, but Osman was the police chief and these details had to be recorded.

'Oh,' he lit a cigarette and blew his nose. 'Oh, that. He went every day to prepare his rice field, though you could see his heart wasn't in it. You know, I could have helped him. I could have spent time with him and he would have felt better, and maybe I would have too. Now I'd give anything to spend time with him and it's too late.'

'The rice field,' Osman reminded him gently.

'I knew he went there in the morning, and one morning I saw someone had actually created a buffalo wallow. They must have really loved that buffalo, I tell you, because someone carried a lot of water from the river over there to make enough mud. It's a real job. It's a lucky buffalo.

'So I saw the mud, and I saw the buffalo, and I knew how to do it so no one would find him until planting, and he'd be unrecognizable for sure.'

'You didn't create it then?' Rahman asked.

'No, what do you think?' Nik Man scoffed. 'The buffalo is supposed to work for you, not the other way around. Do you know how long that must have taken?'

Rahman laughed. 'That's why I looked there! I thought, who'd bother to make a wallow in the dry season except someone with something to hide?'

'It's good thinking, and you'd be right except for this one guy. He just loves the buffalo. I don't get it, but there it is.'

Nik Man shrugged, now thinking about the foibles of over-fond buffalo owners rather than Dris so he cheered up a bit.

'And then?' Osman prompted.

'And then I went to see him and asked him to talk and we walked around. He was so unhappy. He felt so guilty being the reason Salim could attack us both. He was just limp. When we got over to the wallow, I pushed him down into the mud. I apologized as I did it, but he didn't even struggle. He welcomed his death. And now, I'd welcome mine.'

Chapter XXXII

'That's the saddest thing I ever heard,' Rahman said as they led Nik Man into the cell.

'You hear a lot of sad stories in police work,' Osman told him, though he too looked drained. 'Let's sit for a moment before we go in to see Sharifah. I can't face her right away.'

Rahman nodded and two sat facing each other, each looking off into his private space but happy to have the other close by. What a story. Poor Dris. Poor Nik Man. And they still didn't know who'd killed Salim. Right now, Rahman didn't care.

They walked into the other room looking exhausted. The conversation in here had clearly been going in a different direction. There was a look of disapproval on the face of the two older women, Aliza looked preoccupied and Sharifah looked annoyed.

'What happened?' Aliza asked, seeing Rahman's face.

He shook his head and didn't answer.

'So, what's been going on?' Rahman asked.

Maryam sniffed. 'Cik Sharifah knows nothing, sees nothing, remembers nothing. How she gets through the day I don't know.'

'She has admitted to killing the bird at my house,' Maryam said, 'and also bringing Mamat another one because she felt guilty. We thank you for the new bird, which my husband loves,' she told her. 'But I don't know what kind of mind decides to hang a merbok. You'd better think about what kind of person you are. An innocent animal tortured. I don't know what to say.'

'I've apologized, Mak Cik. It was wrong. I felt so guilty, that's why I brought you another. Can't you see I wanted to make it up to you?'

'I see it,' Maryam said flatly, 'but I still need to ask, how could you do it? I believe my nerve would fail me holding a small bird in my hand and then hanging it. You just did it. It doesn't speak well for your character.' Maryam glared at her and Sharifah wisely kept silent.

'We've told her Che Omar has already said she asked him to scare us, but now she's confused,' offered Rubiah.

Osman sat down, unwilling to indulge Sharifah after what he'd just heard. 'So, you didn't ask him?'

'Not in so many words. I think he took it upon himself, thinking it would help me.'

'Really.'

'Yes, and he wanted to get back in my husband's good graces,' she continued. 'Though he would never forgive disloyalty.'

'Really.'

'Yes, Che Osman,' she said with just a touch of the sweetness in her voice giving way to displeasure.

Osman nodded. 'And what did you ask your husband to do?'

'Nik Man? Nothing. I wouldn't ask …'

'Cik Sharifah, I just came from speaking to your husband and it broke my heart. He's haunted by what he did, like …' he tried to find the name of the play it reminded him of, one that he'd struggled through in High School.

'Macbeth,' Aliza provided.

'That's it! Thank you. He's haunted like Macbeth.' This was lost on Sharifah but it seemed a perfect analogy. 'He was forced to murder his best friend by his wife!' He turned to Aliza. 'That's Macbeth, right?' She nodded. Sharifah at this point had gone paler than usual but maintained control of herself.

'I don't know what you're talking about,' she said icily. 'It's nonsense.'

'You're right,' Osman apologized, 'I shouldn't be talking about things like that. But this story was so sad, Rahman and I had to sit down and calm ourselves before we came in here. And even though Nik Man was the murderer, I blame you and your sister.'

'What? I don't know what you're talking about.'

'Alright then, listen. I don't know who thought of it first, you or your sister, but the two of you in the end feared Salim's story would get around, which of course it did. And that when people gossiped about it, they would naturally mention Nik Man, and your family would be shamed, ruined even. And you told Nik Man that he had to kill Dris, who was weak and who would keep people thinking about this gossip. I think you worked on him incessantly.

'Dris was his best friend. He loved Dris, and I don't mean in any other way than how you love a friend. He depended on Dris, they flew kites together and I have no doubt they talked supported each other. *Menyokong padi nak rebah*: they propped

216

up rice plants about to fall. But with Salim telling people that Dris loved Nik Man, well, things changed. Nik Man was afraid you'd leave him. You threatened to leave him, didn't you?'

They waited for Sharifah to defend herself, but she said nothing.

'That's what did it,' Osman continued conversationally. 'He didn't want you to leave him, poor guy. Though now, I think he wishes he made the other choice.'

Sharifah sat up straight and glared at Osman. 'How can you say something like that? You saw how he defends me. He would never regret being with me.'

'Maybe,' Osman said shortly. 'So he killed Dris. He drowned him in the buffalo wallow and then let the buffalo do the rest. But he can't forget it. And we weren't even asking him about Dris. We were asking him about asking Omar to frighten Mak Cik Maryam. But he couldn't control himself. He couldn't stand it. He admitted the whole thing, because he's haunted.'

Maryam and Rubiah were speechless. Aliza put her hand on Rahman's arm. 'That is so sad,' she said.

'It may be sad, but it isn't true,' Sharifah maintained haughtily. 'I never made anyone do anything: not Nik Man, not Omar. People do what they want,' she informed Osman. 'They can blame other people for what they do, but you can't force someone.'

'Did you threaten to divorce him?'

'No.'

'I think you're lying.'

'Well,' she tossed her head, 'I'm not.'

'Did you like Dris?'

'I didn't have that much to do with him. He and Nik Man, they would talk and do kites and all that. He didn't sit and talk to me.'

'Did he come with his wife? Did you visit him and his family?'

'Not really.' She was speaking more normally now. 'It's funny, now that you mention it, you'd think we'd do things together but we didn't. It was just Nik Man and Dris; Latifah and I weren't really involved.'

'Had you heard the rumours about Dris?'

'There's always gossip about one thing and another in a kampong. You know that. I heard something vaguely and asked Nik Man, who laughed. I didn't think much about it after that. I didn't believe it, anyway. They were such close friends, but I didn't think any more was going on between them. I knew Nik Man wasn't that way. I never thought about what way Dris might be. It wasn't something that ever came up.'

'Why then did you worry about gossip? You heard it and didn't believe it. Why did you think anyone else would?'

She sat silent, thinking.

'I think you should know, Cik Sharifah, that what you did isn't against the law. The laws of Malaysia that is; I'm not going to talk about what's right and wrong. But I can't prosecute you for what you did.' Osman looked like he regretted that, and Rahman knew he'd prefer to prosecute Sharifah rather than Nik Man, but the law was clear.

Sharifah gave him a calculating look. 'It doesn't matter, because I didn't do anything.'

'You weren't afraid of gossip?'

'Don't be crazy, or course I was. People would talk about our kids, about us. It would be terrible.'

'Did Bahiyah tell you that?' Maryam asked.

She nodded. 'Yes, because it's true. What the other kids would do to mine at school, I don't even want to think about.'

'What will they do now, when their father's a murderer?'

She looked puzzled, as though this had never occurred to her. Perhaps it never had, because she never thought either of them would ever be caught.

'Well, I don't …'

'Do you think no one will know? It will be the talk of Kelantan. I actually think the other gossip would have faded away, but this is going to go on for some time. And you, will you live with Bahiyah now? Will you remarry, when everyone knows this story?' She licked her lips, but Maryam was relentless. 'Do you think other men will want to marry you after they know what happened to Nik Man? I doubt it.'

'You never planned for any of this when you asked Nik Man to kill his best friend. But tell me, Cik Sharifah; was this your idea or your sister's? I'm curious.'

Sharifah's face crumpled, and she began to cry, more because now she would have real gossip about her in abundance, rather than from regret.

'She told me and I believed her.' She began to sob.

'She hated Dris, didn't she?' Rubiah asked, and Sharifah nodded.

'She thought he took Nik Man away from me, but I laughed at her. It wasn't true. Nik Man loved me, and he could have his own friends. He doesn't need anyone's permission for that. Oh, but after Salim died, she just wouldn't stop, you know. She badgered me day and night, and she made me afraid. I thought people would keep talking about it forever and we'd be part of the same gossip.

'It doesn't make sense to me,' Maryam told her. 'Why such fear? People in Kelantan aren't like that. You know that.'

'Yes, but ...'

'Did she think Dris killed Salim?'

She shook her head. 'Nobody thought that. That's so unlike Dris.'

'Do you think Bahiyah saw this as a way to get rid of Dris, whom she didn't like? While everyone was so worried?' Maryam watched Sharifah for signs of remorse. 'Why did she hate him so much?' She turned to Osman, 'you know, one of the first things she ever said to us was that Dris was no good. Remember, Rubiah?' Rubiah nodded.

'Do you understand why she wanted him dead?'

'She thought Nik Man was too involved with him. She didn't like it.'

'That's it? She'd wanted you to kill him for that?'

Sharifah shook her head, by now she was crying. 'What am I going to do?' she asked. 'Where will I go without Nik Man?' For the second time in as many hours, Osman saw someone bury their head in their hands and surrender themselves to grief. He wouldn't care if he never saw it again.

Chapter XXXIII

Osman sent Sharifah home in a car. He couldn't really prosecute her, and he thought that the situation she created for herself would punish her for years to come. He blamed Bahiyah for it: he knew how much influence Bahiyah had over her younger sister, and in turn how much influence Sharifah had over Nik Man. He mourned the outcome: children growing up without a father, money always being short, and Sharifah forced to depend on the sister she might well end up hating. And poor Nik Man. Osman did not think anyone or anything could punish him with the ferocity with which he was punishing himself. He wasn't being poetic when he said he was haunted, he was being accurate.

None of them could bear any further questioning that night, and Rahman drove Maryam and Rubiah to their respective houses, and went home with his wife. This was one of the first times that Maryam had actually felt that Aliza was gone from the house, and it made her sad. True, she lived close by, and she saw her often, but her daughter was no longer living in her house. She felt that life was fleeting, and she regretted it.

Yi however was still home and still hungry, and supper had to be cooked, and quickly. Work, Maryam believed, was the best cure for depression, and she flung herself into food preparation with a vengeance. Mamat walked in to find onion pieces flying through the kitchen and chicken being hacked without mercy. He quietly backed out of the room and decided to wait for a more auspicious time before talking to her.

At dinner, when Maryam was no longer wielding a cleaver, he asked about the case. 'It's so sad, they've both done wrong and they'll both suffer for it for the rest of their lives. I suppose that's fitting, but I'm worried about Nik Man. I think he may try to harm himself.'

'That bad?' Mamat asked.

'He says he's haunted by the friend he killed. It's a tragedy. I think he's haunted now and he will be all his life. I don't know how you get over something like that.'

'What about his wife?'

'She didn't kill anyone,' Maryam said stiffly. 'I blame her but the person I really blame is her sister Bahiyah, who really made her do it.'

'Made her?'

'I know it sounds strange, but Bahiyah had so much influence over her. I don't understand it myself but it's true.'

'Did you ever find out who killed Salim.'?

Maryam groaned. 'No, not yet. First we solved something we weren't even looking for.'

* * *

Sharifah came back to the police station two hours later, and asked the officer in charge to please let her see her husband. At first he refused, but after she pleaded, he decided he saw no reason really why she couldn't and allowed them both to go into the interrogation room so they could talk. He felt so sorry for her: such a pretty woman and so vulnerable, in such a difficult situation.

Nik Man was looking haggard, and she put a hand up to his cheek, and asked how he was doing. He jerked his head away, something he'd never done before, and looked away from her.

'My life doesn't mean anything anymore,' he announced in a raspy voice, still hoarse from crying. 'I've done the worst thing a man can do. And I see Dris in front of me all the time.

'I only did it for you,' he said sadly. 'I didn't want you to leave me, but I made a mistake. I should have let it happen, and let Dris live. If you left me because if it, I would have seen what kind of person you really are. I've lost you anyway, and I've killed my friend.'

'You haven't lost me,' she cried, reaching for him. 'I'm still here with you, by your side. I won't leave you, I promise.' She expected to see some light of relief, or happiness even, come into his face, but it remained despondent.

'I don't care,' he told her, as she gaped at him. 'I don't want you anymore. I can't see you and not see Dris. I tried after I did it; I tried to be happy that I had you. I told myself I'd made the right decision to save my family. I convinced myself I had chosen well, that I needed you more than I needed Dris, that I loved you and couldn't live my life without you, and our boys.

'But today, when they were asking me questions about it, I

finally allowed myself to see. I asked myself, why do I want a wife who's forced me to do this, and said she'd leave me if I didn't? I sold my soul to keep her. If I refused to do it, would she leave me and return to her sister?

'And I realized, while I was talking to them, what a terrible bargain I'd made. A deal with the devil, that's what it was. Would a wife ask her husband to kill his best friend in order to keep her? No, I thought. Not a wife, but the devil himself.

'I know now what you are, you and your sister, and I wish I'd left you myself and Dris was still alive. All I want is to see Dris again.' He looked at her. 'Not you. I don't want to see you.'

'Are you, are you divorcing me?'

He laughed, a harsh, unforgiving sound. 'Are you listening to me? You're worried about divorce? I'm leaving you forever.' He got up to leave.

Sharifah leapt from her chair and threw her arms around his neck. 'Nik Man, I will wait for you. I wish I had never said anything. I wish I'd never listened to Bahiyah.'

He disentangled himself from her grasp and stepped aside. 'I wish I were dead,' he told her. And then, he left the room.

* * *

Nik Man and Omar were in two cells, which weren't side by side. Rahman thought it best they be separated, but they could still talk between the cells, and Omar was anxious to talk to Nik Man, especially now that he was protected by the bars and Nik Man couldn't choke him.

It was a different Nik Man he saw coming back this evening. He shuffled in, head down, in a way he'd never seen him before. 'What happened?' he asked.

'What do you think?' Nik Man answered. 'I killed Dris. I told them about it. I hope they hang me.'

'No, Nik Man, you must stay optimistic. You may get out of here. You still can live your life.'

'I don't want my life.'

'What a thing to say.'

'Leave me alone.'

'Nik Man,' he began again, 'don't think that way.'

Nik Man lay down and put his arms over his eyes, ignoring Omar. He lay motionless for several minutes, then suddenly asked, 'Did you kill Salim?'

Omar was silent.

'I don't care if you did,' Nik Man said, his eyes still covered. He hadn't moved a muscle except to speak.

'Why?'

'I don't care about much right now. But if you did kill Salim, I'm glad you did. He started all this. I really hate him.' He fell silent again for several minutes. 'It wasn't Dris who killed him, and it wasn't me. I don't think it was his wife: she wanted a divorce, not a murder conviction. Latifah? Unlikely. It leaves you.'

Omar remained silent, his only commentary. He watched Nik Man with sorrow. He thought Nik Man was going mad, not slowly, as often happens, but all at once, as the enormity of what he'd done came home to him. As a bomoh, Omar had treated all manner of mental illnesses, and busied himself diagnosing Nik Man's disease and deciding how to treat it.

He was haunted, that much was clear. Spirit possession, Omar decided, very serious possession by homicidal spirits. Perhaps the spirit of Dris himself, bringing Nik Man, whom he loved, with him in death. *Main Puteri* would be in order: an exorcism to get the spirit out of Nik Man and allow him to live. It would take a while, since this was a serious case. Not only was the spirit possessing Nik Man, but it was doing it with the full collusion of Nik Man's own soul.

Omar could see clearly what happened. Nik Man, his spirit weakened, killed Dris, his close friend. Dris' spirit did not lie quietly under the kerbau: it sought out his killer and his friend, the person he loved above all others. Dris wished to bring Nik Man with him to the afterworld, and his spirit had found no defences in his friend, who yielded to him willingly, almost joyfully.

As a healer it was both his job and his wish to free the spirit of the victim, expel the possessing spirit, and bring his patient back to a more balanced emotional state. He had never before considered this in any previous case, but he wondered in this one if that would be a kindness.

Nik Man might be happier following Dris. As long as he stayed in this world, he'd be overwhelmed with guilt. As he accompanied Dris to the next life, he'd be absolved, forgiven. There was no doubt of that: Dris, in whichever state he was, spirit or corporeal, would forgive Nik Man with all his heart. That relief was not available in this life. He grew cold thinking about it, and thought it would not be long until Nik Man simply ceased living, and joined Dris wherever he was.

Chapter XXXIV

The aftermath of this case was not pretty. Maryam had seldom seen such carnage after a murder, and by now, she'd seen a good deal. Nik Man died three days after being taken into custody, just lying on his bed in his cell, with his arms over his eyes. He had stayed in that position since the night he'd spoken with Omar, and then, one morning, Zul went in with breakfast and he was gone. He lifted his arm and it was stiff and cold, but his face was utterly peaceful.

The last time Osman had spoken with him, when he broke down, his face was a mask of anguish. It comforted both his interrogators to see his face free of suffering. 'It was a blessing for him to die,' Rahman said, and Osman agreed. 'I don't think he wanted to live anymore. I don't think he felt he had anything to live for.'

Maryam thought Sharifah would go mad when she heard Nik Man had died. She began crying, and then in a moment, she stopped, her face expressionless, as though she were carved from stone. She sat quietly, and when Maryam tried to gently lead her from her chair, she resisted. 'I will never be forgiven,' she said to Maryam. 'It's too late for me. I will bear the sin until I die.'

Maryam urged her to pull herself together for her children.

'You must raise, them,' Maryam told her. 'You are both their mother and father now.' Sharifah didn't react except to smile slightly.

'Yes,' she echoed, 'Their mother and father.'

Maryam looked worriedly at Rubiah. 'She's lost her mind,' Maryam whispered. 'She'll die just like her husband.'

Rubiah looked at her critically. 'No she won't,' she said coldly. 'She'll be really upset and then she'll pull herself together and go and live with her sister. The two murderers together. They killed Nik Man as surely as if they'd stabbed him with a *keris*. And now they'll live out their lives explaining to each other how it wasn't their fault.'

'Do you really think so?' Maryam asked. 'She looked so devastated …'

'You said it yourself. She's Bahiyah all over in a different wrapping. Neither of them is going to spend a lot of time thinking about it, once they get over the first shock. Don't worry; she'll take care of her children. She's not going anywhere.'

'I guess for her children's sake I hope you're right.'

'I'm right,' Rubiah said confidently. 'Don't you waste time worrying about her. We'll go and see her in six months and she'll be as good as new.'

* * *

Osman's frustration with this case knew no bounds. He was certain Omar was the killer, and that he had been only too pleased when Sharifah asked him to frighten Maryam. This gave him the excuse he was looking for, and someone else to blame if it came to light, which, as Osman could have told him, things like that always did. But he had no proof. He kept him in jail for as long as he could, but Omar was smart, and had already realized that if he said nothing and stuck to it, Osman would not find anything. He admitted to the spider project, and refused to speak anymore.

It still nagged at Maryam how he knew what she feared. Osman, after his interview with Hatim, told her he was sure it was just coincidence. Hatim knew nothing. 'But Omar told him to use spiders,' she argued. 'He knows. I must find out how he knows.'

She refused to see him in the cells, saying it made her uneasy to be in a small, enclosed space with him. 'He can't conjure spiders out of air,' Osman assured her, but she refused, and Osman did not want to insist. She went into the interrogation room with Rubiah and Aliza, and confronted him.

'You were behind that whole scene at my stall,' she opened the conversation. 'Why?'

'Sharifah asked me to.'

'She didn't tell you exactly what to do, did she?'

He shook his head. 'No, I decided what to do. And then asked that idiot to do it. I don't know why I chose him, honestly. Maybe I wanted to be found out.'

'Then you were successful.'

'We all want to pay for our crimes.'

'In my experience,' Maryam said drily, 'that is definitely not true. Most people would be delighted not to.'

'There's something in us that cries out for forgiveness, and you can't have that if you haven't confessed to what you've done.'

'That's something coming from you,' Rubiah retorted. She shared Osman's conviction that Omar was a murderer, but that proof was not obtainable.

He smiled. 'You're angry at me.'

'I'm tired of you.'

'As am I,' Maryam redirected the conversation. 'But I'm asking you about what you did at my stall.'

'Of course,' Omar replied politely. 'Where were we?'

'You were deciding why you'd chosen Hatim.'

'Ah yes, well, as you can see, a mistake. But I am sorry I did it, and I'm sorry I frightened you.'

'Very politely said,' Maryam acknowledged. 'But tell me, why did you choose to do what you did?'

'Why did I use spiders?'

Maryam didn't like even hearing the word, but she steeled herself to stay still, and stay calm. 'Yes.'

He smiled at her. He knows, she thought. He knows what I fear. 'Mak Cik, many people don't like them. Yes, we hear they helped the Prophet and that we should therefore be kind to them. But still, they look so evil and so strange.' He positively leered at her. 'You know, the way their body is shaped, the legs sticking out, and then the way they skitter about, all those legs …'

Maryam thought she might vomit again, but Aliza put her hand on her back to steady her. She took a deep breath and tried to clear her mind of the picture he drew.

Omar continued, looking pleasant. 'It's a usual thing to be frightened of. Spiders and snakes, right? No one wants them in their lap.' He smiled again, malevolently, and Maryam hated him.

She got to her feet, with Aliza immediately standing behind her to steady her. She did not want to show any weakness before this man.

'Thank you for clarifying,' Rubiah said acidly. 'We are grateful, I'm sure.' She leaned closer to him. 'If I ever see you in the market, or even in Kampong Penambang, I'll make you pay. It's a promise.'

Omar was shocked. He'd never been threatened by a mak cik before. She was venomous. He absolutely believed her. She'd make his life a burden to him if he ever came near them again. He backed away, to stay as far away as possible. He'd avoid her for the rest of his life.

They left, and Maryam said nothing to Osman. Aliza whispered to Rahman, 'He's awful.' Rahman agreed, and only wished he could find some evidence to connect him to the murder. However, he did not, and Osman eventually let him out. Omar knew he'd made a dangerous enemy. *Pelandok lupakan jerat, tapi jerat tak melupakan pelandok:* the deer may forget the trap, but the trap won't forget the deer. Whether Omar remembered it or not, the Kota Bharu Police Department wouldn't forget him, and as soon as they had a chance, they'd pounce.

Chapter XXXV

Maryam found the end of this case unfulfilling. If you found the killer, and you proved it, there was closure, you could see that justice was done and there were not more secrets. She knew, Rubiah knew, the police knew, that Omar had killed Salim, and that they could not prove it was a thorn in everyone's side. The deaths of Dris and Nik Man were tragic, in a way, and Maryam blamed Bahiyah for them, though Bahiyah herself certainly accepted no culpability. *Tempat gajah lalu:* the trail where an elephant has passed, leaving total destruction. The ruin was clear, but the wicked were now going to live their lives without punishment, except for that which their consciences inflicted. Maryam had faint hope those consciences would become particularly active now, having been quiet for so long.

Her depression about this began to lift as Ashikin and Rosnah came closer to giving birth. Ashikin was now complaining of back pains, which she recognized as the harbinger of labour. 'I hope it's a girl,' she confided to her mother. 'It would be nice to have another girl, and it might bring the princess down to earth.'

'It might,' Maryam advised her. 'Or it might just get her going.'

Nuraini, in the meantime, had already laid claim to the baby, and told her mother that she, Nuraini, would be in charge of the baby's care. Ashikin chose to interpret this to mean her daughter was getting over her jealousy, and would now take on the role of big sister. She acknowledged there were other interpretations, which might also fit, but she preferred that one.

Rosnah was jittery, as it was her first child, and Azmi was, to Maryam's surprise, perhaps even more nervous than his wife. He spent long hours with Mamat and Maryam's older brother Malek, soliciting advice on fatherhood, and bringing up many hypothetical scenarios and asking them how he should react. Both finally took him in hand and asked him to calm down, assuring him it would be fine; he'd be an excellent father, a natural.

Maryam found at the end of the case how strange it seemed at first that life continued unimpeded. Salim, Dris and Nik Man were all gone, their families broken, their children fatherless. And yet, Ashikin would have her baby as though nothing had happened, as would Azmi and Rosnah, and all her family seemingly untouched by any of the hatred that had affected so many lives. It was lucky, Maryam thought, that it was her family continuing to grow rather than being shadowed by murder, and she prayed for their on-going good fortune.

Now, if only Yi would fill out …

Read the next book in the
Kain Songket Mysteries series

TOP SPINNING (VOL. 5)

Top spinning isn't for children in Kelantan: burly men hurling large heavy tops wrapped with thick cord compete for the longest spin, with significant money riding on the outcome. One of these throws leads to murder, and Mak Cik Maryam follows the trail. A murderer at large from a previous case continues to haunt her, and her determination to finally bring the killer to justice and solve this more recent crime puts her in danger, but does not dissuade her.

SHADOW PLAY (VOL. 1)

Shadow Play is the first in the series of Kain Songket Mysteries set in the northern state of Kelantan, Malaysia, during the 1970s. Mak Cik Maryam, a *kain songket* (silk) trader in Kota Bharu Central Market, discovers a murder in her own backyard, shattering the bucolic village world she thought surrounded her. While the new Chief of Police, a pleasant young man from Ipoh whose mother's admonitions about the wiles of Kelantanese girls still ring in his ears, wrestles with the bewildering local dialect, Maryam steps up to solve the mystery herself. Her investigation brings her into the closed world of the *wayang kulit* shadow play theater and the lives of its performers—a world riven by rivalries and black magic. Trapped in a tangle of jealousy, Maryam struggles to make sense of the crime in spite of the spells sent to keep her from secrets long buried and lies woven to shield the guilty.

• Winner - Best Debut Novel
SBPA Book Awards (Singapore, 2012)

• Shortlisted - English Fiction
Popular–The Star Readers' Choice Awards (Malaysia, 2013)

PRINCESS PLAY (VOL. 2)

Mak Cik Maryam is plunged once again into the shadowy world of murder, hatred and madness when a fellow market woman is killed after a successful *main puteri* (princess play) curing ceremony. Suddenly, the villagers she thought she knew reveal secrets she never suspected, while her good sense and solid courage lead her to unmask the murderer among them. Follow Mak Cik Maryam in the second Kelantanese murder case in the Kain Songket Mysteries series.

• Shortlisted - English Fiction
Popular–The Star Readers' Choice Awards (Malaysia, 2014)

SPIRIT TIGER (VOL. 3)

Tiger spirits prowl Kampong Penambang in the third novel of the award-winning Kain Songket Mysteries detective series set in Kelantan, Malaysia. Amateur sleuth Mak Cik Maryam volunteers to investigate the death of a village reprobate, convinced it will be a quick investigation with clear suspects. But her detection soon spirals out of control with a plethora of suspects who wanted him dead, including almost everyone he knew. Maryam falls victim to a *hala* spell turning her into a were-tiger, terrifying her and her family, and leaving her vulnerable to any number of evil influences. Join Mak Cik Maryam in her latest adventure, *Spirit Tiger*, as she investigates Kelantan's gambling underworld.